THURSBITCH

Alan Garner is one of Britain's outstanding authors. He has won many prizes for his writing and in 2001 was awarded the OBE for services to literature. His books include *The Owl Service* (which won the *Guardian* Award and the Carnegie Medal), *Red Shift* and *The Stone Book Quartet*, recognised by the Phoenix Award of America.

Alan Garner

THURSBITCH

VINTAGE

Published by Vintage 2004

2 4 6 8 10 9 7 5 3 1

Copyright © Alan Garner 2003

Alan Garner has asserted his right under the Copyright,
Designs and Patents Act, 1988 to be identified as the author
of this work

First published in Great Britain in 2003 by
The Harvill Press

Vintage
Random House, 20 Vauxhall Bridge Road,
London SW1V 2SA

Random House Australia (Pty) Limited
20 Alfred Street, Milsons Point, Sydney
New South Wales 2061, Australia

Random House New Zealand Limited
18 Poland Road, Glenfield,
Auckland 10, New Zealand

Random House (Pty) Limited
Endulini, 5A Jubilee Road, Parktown 2193,
South Africa

The Random House Group Limited Reg. No. 954009
www.randomhouse.co.uk/vintage

A CIP catalogue record for this book
is available from the British Library

ISBN 0 099 45936 1

Chapter heads drawn by
Griselda Greaves

Papers used by Random House are natural, recyclable
products made from wood grown in sustainable forests.
The manufacturing processes conform to the environ-
mental regulations of the country of origin

Printed and bound in Great Britain by
Cox & Wyman Limited, Reading, Berkshire

For Tatiana Dobronitskaya

&

Richard Morris

and nu wið Grendel sceal,
wið þam aglæcan ana gehegan
ðing wið þyrse.

And now I've got a bone to pick
With knacker master Grendel;
Yon Big Thing.

Beowulf: ll.424–426

***

Ac ther ne was wye non so wys that the way thider couthe,
But blostrede forth as bestes ouer baches and hulles,
Til late was and longe that thie a lede mette,
Yparayled as a paynyem in pylgrimes wyse.

But no one was near as knew the next way.
They blunder about same as beasts, by the valleys and hills,
While it is gone late and long past; a lommocking youth,
A heathen in harness, they meet; he's a wandering sort of a chap.

Piers Plowman: C. (ed. Derek Pearsall),
Passus VII, ll. 158–161

***

With the drawing of this Love and the voice of this Calling

Little Gidding: V, 25

Go back. What was must never be.

1

He climbed from Sooker and the snow was drifting. He held Jinney's reins to lift her, and Bryn ran round the back of Samson, Clocky and Maysey, nipping their heels so that they would not drag on the train. They passed Ormes Smithy, up Blaze Hill and along Billinge Side.

> "O come all ye wych wallers as have your salt to sell.
> I'll have you give good measure and skeer your vessels
> well.
> For there's a day of reckoning, and Hell will have its share;
> Old Nick will take you by your necks,
> As Mossy ketched his mare."

The wind was full in their faces and the horses were trying to tuck into the bank for shelter, but Bryn kept them from shoving their panniers against the rocks. Now it was dark and the snow was swarming into his lanthorn and he could not see for the whiteness; but he knew the road.

"Eh. Jinney. Can you tell me this poser? 'Luke had it in front. Paul had it behind. Phoebe Mellor had it twice in the middle afore she was wed. Lads have it. Wenches don't. Yon's in life, but not in death'."

The bells of her collar jingled as she shook her mane, but she followed his voice in the snow.

They crossed the four-went-way and began the drag up Pike Low. Here the wind filled his eyes and nostrils and he had to suck at his beard so that the hair would not be ice around his mouth. By Deaf

[1]

Harry the lead horse felt it, even though it was up the moor, and she reared, whinnying through her muzzle. He shortened the rein and patted her neck and shoulder. She was striking out with her front hooves.

"Nay, Jinney, nay, lass. Yon's a high stone, that's all. He can't hurt you. He can't move, choose what Tally Ridge'll say. Well, not tonight he won't."

He braced for the top of Pike Low.

"Blood and elbows!"

The back end of Pike Low down to Blue Boar was the sharpest in all the hills, however the storm should go. If it was behind, it came round Billinge or out of Rainow hole. North, it came over Sponds. East, it mounted on Windgather. And south it upped past Shuttlingslow and along Lamaload. There was no getting from it. But Thoon was worst, and this was it.

"Oh, what a world. What a world. Summer hangs in a bag tonight, Jinney. Right enough. But we shall fettle it, shan't we? We shall that."

He led the train down from Pike Low by Drakeshollow; the wind and the snow still in his face.

"Eh, Jinney. Have you ever thought?"

He was talking to stop his skin from freezing in its white mask and to keep the train calm.

"Have you ever thought who made all this here? And whatever for?"

He checked to his left that he was on his track and saw a glim of light, which would be the candle in the window at Blue Boar.

"Come up, Jinney. Come up. Come up, lass. Nearly there. And what was at the start? There's no use in asking them lot down Saltersford. They'd put a hat on a hen, they would. They'd daub a house with a hammer. They'd plough a rock, them and their ways. Them as crack on as how they know all sorts. Them as broke Jenkin."

The horses were blowing. He had to keep talking, or they would not make the hill. But they would follow his voice. What he said did not matter; it did not matter: not to them.

"Well, that lot, once them preachifiers, once them lot gets hold, there's neither end nor side to 'em. They must have it as how first was their roaring chap, and he was, like, borsant with being by himself. Ay. So he made all this here. But you ask 'em where the chap was agen he'd finished: did he stand or did he sit? And if he's standing, where's the floor? And if he's sitting, where's his arse? Or was he in bed or what? And they'll land in such a festerment they'll big dog you. I've seen 'em. But what right have they to tell Bull what to be doing? Them as have it all writ, and ever sin they got to shutting sky in a box of walls and stuck a lid on it same as it was a suit o' coffin stuff, and then think as they can tell Bull, by the god!"

The anger added to his strength.

"As the fool thinks, so the bell clinks. I don't know. Let there be light! Yay. But if there were no sun moon stars nor tickmijigs, what's the odds? No. I'll tell you as how a youth on market once told it me, if I understand him aright. Mind you, where he got it from, I can't tell you. Some market else, I'll be bound. But now then. Hearken ye. This youth, he says, at start, there were Night and Mither. That's all it took. Night and Mither. And when Night and Mither met, it stands to reason as how there'd be these here clag-arsed journeys to be tholed. Night and Mither, Jinney; them didn't have to own from nowhere."

They climbed up Ewrin Lane and over Waggonshaw Brow by Buxter Stoops. As he passed through the farmyard, he saw Martha Barber at the curtain sack of her window.

"Is it you, Jagger Turner?"

"Ay, but it is, Widder Barber!"

"I thought I heard. Will you come thy ways?"

"Nay, Missis. But thank ye. If I let this lot melt I'd starve to death."

"Hast any piddlejuice about you for such a time?"

"I have and all. Good to make a cat speak and a man dumb. Pass us your jug."

She unbolted the door and opened it enough for her to hand him a small jug. Then she bolted the door. He filled the jug.

"Get that down you, Missis."

She opened and closed the door at a snatch.

"I always say as how there never has been nowt like your piddlejuice, Jagger; and that's a fact!"

"Ay, Missis! If you're on the road all hours in these hills, you must be fit for owt, or you'll find it's when bum hole's shut, fart's gone. It's there, you know. Oh, ah. When bum hole's shut, fart's gone."

They laughed on either side of the door.

"Give us a tune, Jagger! I feel a little ditty coming on me and I've a flavour for to sing it."

"Nay, Widder Barber. I must be getting down bank, and me beasts need their rest."

He saw her shadow. She was hopping and began to dance. Her voice was uncertain at first, but then it broke forth with a strength that not even the wind could quell.

> "O, the first great joy of Mary Anne
> It were the joy of one:
> To see her own son little Jack
> To suck at her breast bone;
> To suck at her breast bone the blood
> From out his father's thigh.
> Euoi! Euoi! Io! Euoi!
> Through all Eternity!"

"I must be getting down bank, Widder Barber! The wind's in

Thoon, and me beasts'll be bangled if they're not moving!"

Martha Barber was now leaping in her dance.

    "The second great joy of Mary Anne
     It were the joy of two:
     To see her own son little Jack
     Inside o' th' bull to go;
     Inside o' th' bull to go for them
     To shed for him to be.
     Euoi! Euoi! Io! Euoi!
     Through all Eternity!"

He led the team into the road and set off from Buxter Stoops on its ridge and down the bank towards Saltersford. The lane was so steep that it had cut the hill, but any shelter it gave was of no use against the snow. He waded into the drift, thrashing right and left to make a softer, wider way for the team. The hollering wind took Martha Barber's voice from him, but the song was now in the storm itself and came to him out of Thoon's very own mouth.

    "The next great joy of Mary Anne
     It were the joy of eight:
     To see her own son little Jack
     Go down again to Fate;
     Go down again to Fate and drink
     Death deeper nor the sea.
     Euoi! Euoi! Io! Euoi!
     Through all Eternity!"

He led them round the Nab End three-went corner, past Great Lowes; and Edward was not in bed. Now the lane was level, for the valley. He opened a pannier, took out a handful of salt and put it in his pocket. Then he closed the pannier and moved along the line of the team, rubbing the noses of each: Samson, Clocky, Maysey.

"Go thy ways, Jinney."

He checked the buckles and bants.

"See them home, Bryn. I must do right by Nan Sarah. And by the stars. And then. Be good, Bryn."

2

The people filed out of the chapel into the snow. The catch of the sun lessened the stifle of coals in the stone walls. The air nipped.

"Spirit was in thee today, Dickun," said Clonter Oakes.

"The Lord trod mightily upon my tongue," said Richard Turner. "Now let's be doing to fetch that young youth home."

Edward Turner joined them. Clonter set off down Flake Pits, but Richard Turner called him back.

"We must go by Nab End."

"This is aimest."

"Yay."

They took the lane past Saltersford and Great Lowes to Nab End three-went.

"There's been me and Ridges this road," said Edward. "See at foot marks."

"He's up bank," said Richard Turner.

"Up bank?" said Edward. "He'll not be up bank in this, Father. It's deep as owt."

Clonter lifted his arm.

"Hearken."

"What?" said Richard Turner.

"Hearken ye."

In the air there was the small sound of bells, jingling twice, above the drift-filled way.

"It's him," said Edward. "Daft beggar."

They floundered through Ewrin Lane. It was a powder of ice, scarcely hollowed from the unbroken snow.

"Here," said Clonter.

He had come to a recess, an overhang of the wind, and in it a body was showing dark. It was the lead horse of a train; and it was alive. Richard Turner checked it and moved on. A dog yelped.

"There's another," said Clonter.

"Leave them. They'll thole," said Edward. "There must be two more. Come up! Come up!" He whistled. The dog yelped again.

"I've got 'em," said Richard Turner, without pausing. He forced himself through the crests.

"Where's Jack?"

"Where he was shaping to be."

They found him sitting against Osbaldestone below Buxter Stoops above the three-went. He was clarted with snow to his shoulders. Frost silvered each hair of the black goatskin. His arms stretched out to hold. His skin crackled yellow, and ice clad his beard, mouth, nose and eyes. The eyes were wide; and the dog lay by him and licked his face.

"Eh up. He's laughing."

"He's not that."

"Shut his een, Dickun."

"No. Let him see. Worser had he flit; more better has he found."

"You reckon?"

"Blood's forever at a three-went."

Edward leaned across and folded the lids. Splinters fell.

"He'll do," said Richard Turner.

"Poor as a rook."

"I said he'll do."

"Look ye. On the stone here," said Edward. "It's all over honey."

"Never," said Clonter. "Them days are done."

"Anyroad, it's sweet."

"Then whatever's this?"

"Nowt." Richard Turner reached forward and brushed the snow with his hand. It made a mark on the white.

"What is it?"

"I said: nowt."

"But I saw," said Edward.

"You didn't see nowt," said Richard Turner. "Be told."

"I did see. I did that," said Clonter. "It was a woman's."

"I saw it," said Edward. "I saw."

"Footprint. Just one. Print of a woman's shoe."

3

"The map doesn't say we must keep to the path."

The way along the ridge was strung with walkers in both directions, urging themselves on their trekking poles.

"Let's get into Cheshire," he said. "It's quiet there." He pressed down the tangled sheep wire between a break in the walls so that she could cross the boundary.

At once they were on blanket bog and cotton grass. Behind them woollen hats bobbed for a while. The wind was the same, but there was a stillness that the path did not have. Their feet squeezed peat water from the clumps and they kept falling between and catching each other; but it was their own pace at last. Hang gliders, jumping from the scarp of Old Gate Nick, drifted away over Saltersford and down Todd Brook.

They were below the ridge, on a shelving plateau, and beyond was the dark side of Andrew's Edge, and, in between, a luminous air above the hidden valley. They plodded over the sprung land.

"Fantastic," she said.

They were on the lip.

"Fan. Tastic."

"Yes."

"No. That."

It was a cube of rock sticking out of the peat a little below them. Its back was buried, its top flat and tilted to give a launch out across the valley. The sides were layered bands, disturbed by running cracks.

The front was an arch, and all was hollow within; a cave, a hive, an oven, curved round, with more layers lying on each other, and at the back an upright crevice in the crag, going into the ridge but not through the slab of roof nor through the slab of floor.

"It's classic."

"More Gothic. It's not on the map."

"Textbook Namurian. Chatsworth Grit."

"We're nowhere near Chatsworth."

"You're being stupid." She moved around the rock. Her hands read every layer and fissure, caressed the ripples on the outside of the top and the smooth floor within. "My God, my God, I know this. Marsdenian R-Two."

"Go on."

"It's a dream," she said. "The recessed eroded scarp face and the dip slope."

He followed her.

"And the sides. Freeze-thaw joints opening up on the bedding planes, and some cross bedding. The base of the trough. Am I gabbling?"

She looked at him, her hand stilled on the rock.

"No. No. Go on."

She smiled, excited, nervous. Her hand moved.

"The freeze-thaw doesn't penetrate through, nor does the sub-vertical master joint. Which suggests. Wait. Wait. I know. The master joint can't be tectonic. So the horizontal layered joints have developed weaknesses in the bedding and the cross bedding by freeze-thaw processes. Which means. Am I still making sense?"

"Of course."

"Really?"

"Keep going."

"Right. Which means the weaknesses are stress phenomena. So the sediments would have been about three kilometres below the sea floor at the time. There's forestepping here. And here's a trace of the palæoslope."

"Stop now."

They had worked around to the top of the rock.

"What's wrong?" she said.

"Nothing. Absolutely nothing. You were terrific."

"Was I?"

"Promise."

"Did I get it right?"

"You began to rev, that's all."

He looked out over the valley, the one ruin of house below, Andrew's Edge beyond.

"Give me your hand, fair maiden," he said. "Come and be Cinderella."

She took his hand and stepped up to the ledge.

"This mark. Put your foot in. There. A perfect fit. So you shall go to the ball."

"That, you idiot, is a transient artefact of weathering in the laminate."

"Well, it fits your foot, *en passant*, as it were."

They laughed, and went to the cave. They sat on the smooth floor, which made a canopied chair for them, holding them.

"Are you sure it's natural?"

"Positive."

They were silent. The wind. Distant sheep.

"There's a front moving in," he said. "Shall we be getting on?"

"Not yet. I want it all."

Silent.

"You can see for ever from here," he said.

"It depends which way you see it."

"A womb with a view."

"Don't even think of starting that one," she said.

"Sorry. Freudian lisp."

"Ian!"

"Ah well. Another damp squid. Cheer up."

"I'm not down. There's so much. If you know how to look."

"Show me," he said.

"Well. For instance. How far is it to that next ridge?"

He took the map and measured. "About one point two five kilometres."

She spread her hands on her knees. "Got a calculator?"

"Somewhere."

"One point two five kilometres," she said. "Watch this. Divide a million by eleven point two five and multiply by one point two five."

"Good Lord. It's exactly one hundred and eleven thousand one hundred and eleven point one recurring."

"Neat."

"You knew!"

"Of course I didn't know. But I like it. Apt."

"So what does that tell us?" he said.

She moved her gaze from her hands to Andrew's Edge. "We both look, but we see differently."

"Meaning?"

"You call it a view. But it's a song. Such a dance. If I sat and didn't move for one hundred and eleven thousand one hundred and eleven years, according to you, these fingernails would grow as far as that ridge. Everything's moving. When here was under the water, it was south of the Equator. And ever since, all of it's been travelling at about eleven point two five kilometres every million years. It's still doing it. Here is just where it happens to have got to now. That's the song. Pangæa. Gondwanaland. The song and the dance."

"What's that about your fingernails?"

"It's another part of the song. Our nails grow at the same rate as continental drift."

He smiled, but she did not.

"There's the beauty. If we could only dance more, for longer." She stood up. "Instead of games. Just word games." Her eyes were bright. "But that would be selfish. Wouldn't it?"

"Oh, perispomenon!"

He had been tracing the line of the vertical crack at the back of the cave while she spoke.

"I've been stung!"

"Don't move. The bee's all right. It's still attached."

"I know it's attached!"

"Keep still. Don't hurt it."

She held the bee so that it could not fly. Then slowly, gently, she turned it on his skin until the sting was free. She looked at the bee to check. "There. Off you go. No harm done."

"I'm harmed!"

"Spray it with some of that anti-histamine from your bag of tricks," she said. "And let's walk."

A track cut down across the steep of the valley, brown on green, more than a path. It had been made, though rough; too mean and rushy to walk, but the bank thrown up to the side was firm enough to wobble on.

She put her arm through his.

"It still hurts."

"You'll live."

"This track isn't marked, either."

"But it's here. So you can put the map away and watch the real thing. Then you won't sprain your ankle. How's the hand?"

"Anaphylactic shock can be fatal. Do you think it's swelling?"

"You tell me. I know you will."

The track turned back on itself off the rough onto a more lush pasture sliced by gullies, reed lined and wet. Water gurgled all around and they splashed over stones towards a ruin higher up the brook, and the track merged with another, more broken, nearer the house.

"There's a way out, up to the watershed, along that line of wall," he said. "It's nothing but benchmarks."

They clambered about the ruin: two gable ends of stone, stone wall footings, rotten spars and beams, holes of windows, some still spanned by lintels of twisted, weathered, silver oak, as if a part of something else. Fallen masonry and rubble masked the flagstones. There were gateposts and traces of outbuilding. A silted-up tank, made from four slabs, collected the brown water that ran off the surface above and seeped towards the brook.

He checked on the map. "Thursbitch."

They crossed the brook at a ford. The main flow came from the head of the valley, and a feeder had cut through the shale to join it. At the point where they met, the bank was higher, and on it a stone.

"This one's odd," she said. She ran her hands over it and looked closely. "The sedimentary structures are quite different. And it's too big for a post; the wrong shape. That top feature has some strong stylisation."

"Doctor Malley," he said, "is there anything at all that you do not know?"

She looked at him.

"Let's find those benchmarks of yours."

She set off across the reed bog. He plunged after her, to her. They both fell together in the mire, on their knees, black splashing to their faces, hands under the water.

"Sal. I'm sorry. I am so sorry."

She pulled a face, and banged her forehead against his in the green reed light and the cotton grass. "Just get me up, somehow; or we'll be here all night."

He pulled a hand out, and slipped sideways. She caught hold of his sleeve and hauled herself over him, laughing. "People pay good money to watch this sort of thing." They wrestled each other till they stood. "Shit and Derision. Trees. The trees. Over there."

The reeds were high. But beyond was a patch of other ground, and the scraggy tops of thorn trees showed, a poor cluster beside the brook. They rinsed their hands and faces in the water.

"Shall we go back?" he said.

"We must find your benchmarks. Where are they?"

"In the wall up there."

"Come on, then. And what's that?"

A circle of marsh ate at the bank, and on the far side there was an arch of stone.

They moved towards it on sheep walks. It was not a house of any kind, but a structure that had collapsed into the hill. Most of it was covered by a single broken and massive flag that had been its roof. Under it were low walls.

"Are those steps?" he said. "There's water running." He took out his torch and pushed it between a crack. "See anything?"

"No," she said. "Yes. It's a spring. Or a well of some sort. The steps go down to it. There's a channel cut. The water's coming out of the hill. It looks absolutely clear. Then it must drain out to the marsh. What does it remind you of?"

"Nothing."

"Not that?" She pointed up to the ridge across the brook. The rock outcrop was opposite them, on the horizon, from where they stood; the only break in the smooth long line of hill.

"But this has been made," he said.

"Then there'd be no point in building the other well for the farm. If this is good water, they wouldn't have put up with that muck for the sake of a few metres."

They left the well and found the wall. Whole lengths of it were no more than two courses high, and in places there were only gaps and lines in the thin soil.

"The first one should be just beyond a sheepfold," he said. "I'm going to complain about this map. That well's not shown, either. The one at the farm is."

They came to the remnant of a wooden enclosure lying against the drystone wall.

"It's in the right place for the sheepfold. Look for a benchmark in about one hundred and fifteen metres. It'll be on something obvious that can't be shifted easily."

"Like this?"

It was another big stone, a pillar set in the wall, with a hole running through.

"That'll be it. Where's the benchmark?"

"I can't see one."

They pulled the grass down to where the stone met the ground.

"Nothing."

"The next should be about one hundred and ninety metres."

They tramped up beside the wall.

It was another holed stone, and this time pointed at the top. There was no benchmark.

"I can't see any function for these big stones," she said. "Walls aren't built that way."

"There should be one more at the watershed. How are you feeling?"

"Fine. Nearly dry. How's the hand?"

"It still hurts."

"You poor thing."

They followed the wall. Another tall holed stone was where it should be. Something had broken it off at its base and it lay on the ground; but again no mark.

"Have some glucose." He offered her a tablet. "Do you want to go back, or shall we pick up the ridge at Shining Tor?"

"Back. I'm intrigued."

"By what?"

"The whole place. Look at it."

"It's a terrific – ?"

"View," she said. "I'm not all Upper Carboniferous."

4

"Hic, hoc, the carrion crow,
The carrion crow I see.
As I walk by mysen
And I talk to mysen,
Mysen says unto me:
Look to thysen,
Take care of thysen,
For nobody cares for thee."

Jack climbed out of Goyt by Embridge Causey, over Withenlach and passed through Old Gate Nick. The road dropped straight to Saltersford.

"Hic, hoc, the carrion crow,
The carrion crow I see.
I talk to mysen
And I say to mysen,
In the sen-same nominy:
Look to thysen,
Or not to thysen,
The sen-same thing shall be.
Hic, hoc, the carrion crow,
The carrion crow's for me."

He went down the road over Shudder Brow and Hog Brow Top, along by the high stones, and rested at Shady to take in the valley.

"Home now, me lass."

The lead horse shook her mane and the bells rang.

He saw the men below him, mowing The Halls. Higher Hall and Lower Hall had been cut, and the team was in Little Hall. He saw his father and Edward, and Clonter Oakes had come from Green Booth, and Sneaper Slack had come from The Dunge, and Tally Ridge from Hulley Hey; and the Lomas women were tedding the swaths as they fell.

The mowers paused to whet, and the stones' ringing on the blades carried to him in the quietness. He cupped his hands to his mouth.

"Hic! Hoc! The carrion! Crow!"

They heard him and waved. He waved his stick. The cows on Todd Hill lifted their heads. He started down the last stretch.

"The carrion crow! The carrion crow! The carrion crow!"

Mary and Nan Sarah ran out into the yard and swung their aprons. He whirled his hat high. The feather caught the sun. The farm dogs barked, and Bryn answered them.

He stopped in the yard, loosened the panniers and put them in the brewis, fed and watered the horses and went into the houseplace to the table. Mary was by the fire. Nan Sarah came to him, holding a mug of buttermilk. He drained it at a swig, and Nan Sarah sat on his knee. They kissed.

"Now then, our Jack," said Mary. "Where hast tha bin this journey?"

"Oh," he answered, as he always did, "up a-top of down yonder, miles-endy-ways, tha knows, at Bog o' Mirollies, where cats kittlen magpies." They laughed; his bigness filled the room.

"What have you fetched us?" said Nan Sarah. It was all a part of the game.

"Fetched you?" said Jack. "And why should a man be fetching things for the likes of you? It's enough for a man to walk from Derby, without being mithered with fetching. I could sup some more buttermilk."

Nan Sarah brought the mug again, excited. Jack took the satchel from round his neck and put it on the table.

"But who knows?" he said. "Who knows what's in the old powsels and thrums? Ay. Now then. What have we here?" He felt around among the contents of the satchel. "Powsels and thrums. Powsels and thrums. No. It seems there's nowt of consequence. Eh up. Wait on." He took out a lace bonnet and threw it across to Mary. "There's that. I got it off a chap from Nottingham way."

Mary put the bonnet on, crimped it with her fingers, turning her head from side to side. "How's it look?" she said.

"It suits you well, Ma Mary."

"What's for me?" said Nan Sarah.

"What's for you? I don't know. I do not." He felt around again. "Powsels and thrums. Powsels and thrums. Eh up. There's this here dishclout."

He proffered the grubby rag.

"Now see as you don't drop it. They come expensive, do dish-clouts."

He put it into her hand.

"It's a weight," she said. "What's in it?"

"A dog turd, I shouldn't wonder."

She unfolded the cloth.

"Oh, Jack. Whatever is this?"

It was a stone cup. A hollowed stone cup. Outside it was rough rock melted wax, grey, yellow, dark. Inside was polished deep with crystals white blue purple.

"Hold it against the sun," he said.

The rough rock glowed from the colours within.

"Jack, it's gorgeous."

"Down Derby, they call them 'grallusses'. Leastways, that's what the chap I got it from said. But he could've been twitting me. What took my fancy is the way as how, one road, it's nowt, and t'other road, it's all sorts."

[21]

"What's it of?" said Nan Sarah.

"Blue John."

"And what's that?"

"Stone as is found at Castleton, and nowhere else in all the wide world, so they say. You'd think, if that's true, it'd be worth more nor gold nor silver. But I got it for a hoop of salt. Nobbut a hoop."

"Blue John," said Sarah.

"Am I?"

"You boiled turmit. But what's it for?"

"I never asked."

"Eh," said Mary. "You two. There's men yonder as are at making a right job; when you've nowt better."

Jack went into the brewis and picked up a two-gallon jar in each hand and walked down to The Halls. The team saw him and straightened their backs from the mowing.

"Look ye," said Sneaper. "Here comes trouble. Here comes a young tragwalleter as never did a hand's turn in his life."

Jack laughed, and sat in the shade of the wall. The men sat with him, and he passed the ale jars around. The women went further along, by themselves.

"And what do you call this here effort?" he said. "It's never mowing. Three fields not done yet? Whenever did you start? After you'd had your dinners?" He took a stalk and chewed the joint of the stem. "By. But it's sweet. Are you not being previous, Father?"

"I thought we might as good try to get a second bite," said Richard Turner, "if we took his head off now."

"Yay," said Jack. "And I might as good milk ducks. But think on. There's my hay, too. And it's to be High Medda stuff. Rye. And I don't want it in next Monday-come-never-on-a-wheelbarrow. I do not. My beasts pay their pasture. So don't none of you stop mowing afore you see a star."

[22]

"Best be doing," said Richard Turner. He lifted his sickle, and from the band of his hat he took a stem of grass and fixed it in Jack's hat, on the other side from the feather. "And then."

Jack looked at him; and nodded.

The men went back to their line, and sharpened up.

"What've you fetched?" said Tally Ridge.

"Malt," said Jack.

"Shall you let us have a gallon?"

"We'll have to see. Most of it's spoken for at Chester."

"When shall you be back?" said Tally.

"Time enough," said Jack. "When have I ever not?"

5

The valley lay in scudding sunshine: browns and greens and browns and greens and browns.

They returned along the wall. The wind was behind them, from the south, and the low cloud caught them before they were aware, and they were in a glittering mist worse than fog. The valley had gone.

"Keep to the wall, Sal. We'll drop through this."

It was easy at first. The wall took them to the stone. But the chill had lingered in their clothing and the mist was cold.

"There's a gap here," she said. "I can't see the next bit."

"It'll be there. Look. What did I tell you?"

"It's another of those stones."

"Same thing."

"It's not the same. It's by itself. There is no wall."

"There has to be."

"There doesn't have to be. And there isn't," she said.

"That is no problem."

"I can see someone."

It was another tall stone.

"It is no problem," he said. "The GPS will give us a fix." He took it out of his bag and put it on the stone. "Leave it a minute or two to scan."

They waited.

"Is it switched on?" she said.

He looked at the screen.

"Did you put batteries in?"

"It's not picking up on the satellites. The valley may be too steep. But we can't be far off the line of the wall." He took out the compass and the map. "If the worst comes to the worst, we can do it by dead reckoning."

They moved away from the stone, holding hands; she finding a way, he following the bearing. When they came to reed beds they forced themselves through to keep the line. Everywhere was silence.

"I can hear the brook," she said.

"Steady."

They were at running water.

"It's the main brook," she said. Water came in from the left. "Here's where we crossed." They went over the water.

"And here's the path," he said.

"Make sure it's the right one."

"It's that rough stretch we were on after we'd come down from the rock and before we reached the farm."

"We haven't passed the well, and we haven't passed the farm," she said.

"They could have been three metres away and we'd have missed them."

"And no trees, either. Ian? I think it's safe to say. We. Are. Lost."

"This path's bearing eleven degrees west of where we should be."

"So much for your gismos. I'm following what we've got. Someone's used it. It'll go somewhere."

"The compass says we should be dropping, and we're not. We're climbing."

They came to another big stone, tall, narrow; but this was a part of a gateway, though there was no gate, and there was a wall to right and to left. The track led through.

"Glucose," she said, and sat against the stone.

They sucked the tablets.

"The quiet's different now. Hear it."

"There's some chocolate," he said.

"Shh. Listen."

"Up there?"

"Higher."

They were whispering.

"The cloud's thinning."

Through the streaks that came and went they could see that they were above the brook. The other side of the valley was close. Small bells tinkled.

"There!"

A rift in the cloud showed a man climbing above them. He wore a black coat that came almost to the ground, and a hat over long hair. He was bearded.

"Hello!"

There was a lurcher at his heels, and he held a rope on which there were four horses, one behind the other, draped with panniers, and on the neck of the lead horse was a frame from which bells hung.

"Hello! Hello!"

The rift closed.

"Hello!"

It opened again for a moment. The man had seen them, but he did not stop. He shouted something and pointed with his stick back to the way he had come, then the cloud joined again. A dog barked.

"On your feet, Doctor Malley."

The light was blue above, and the hillside cleared. Pockets of mist lifted out of hollows and streamed up the gullies.

"I told you." They looked back along the valley. "There's the farm. And the track going up to the rock. I can see the trees near that well or whatever. There aren't any others. And we are: here." He checked the map with the compass. "We've been on this path all the time. Rum. It was definitely eleven degrees off, back there. You can get pockets of geomagnetic anomaly; but I should not have expected it here."

"Where's the man with the horses?" she said.

"He'll be on the ridge somewhere."

The path rose to the shoulder of the field and over the brow. The land opened up and they were out. Todd Brook fell to its broad main bed at Saltersford, and their way took them across through the yard of Howlersknowl, dipped and lifted again to the gate to the road from Jenkin Chapel up to Pym Chair. They crossed the cattle grid.

The road was steep and low between wall-topped banks. The model flyers at Pym Chair were still wiggling their remote controls, and the coloured wings were jousting with each other and the air.

"Time to go," she said. "This place has had enough of us."

6

Jack wiped his mouth and beard with his neckcloth and poured himself another mug. "I'm for Thursbitch on a job of me father's. Are you coming?"

"Who? Me?" said Nan Sarah.

"Well, it's not me," said Mary. "I doubt there's more to Thursbitch in that one's reckoning."

"I'll get me shawl, then," said Nan Sarah.

"What you want's in the brewis," said Mary. "Under the slopstone."

Nan Sarah left the houseplace and came back with her shawl wrapped loosely about her.

"Are you fit?" she said.

Jack and Nan Sarah walked up the Old Gate and turned off to the right, aslant the Butts. The Butts was the last field. The way went through the corner, and then the valley showed. On one side, from Cats Tor to Shining Tor, the ridge was in sunlight; and on the other was Andrew's Edge, dark always after the morning. Todd Brook fed from the springs of the peat and came together at the ford.

High stones marched into Thursbitch from all around, gathering the ways from the hills down and through the valley: from Longclough, from Osbaldestone, from Jenkin, each to be seen by another, but none by all, marking every brink; Two-Johnny Goiker on Andrew's Edge, and Sprout-kale Jacob over Redmoor; Biggening Brom under Catstair; each line and double way coming to Bully Thrumble at the fork at the ford below Thoon. And Lankin stood at the mouth.

"Where are we going?" said Nan Sarah.

"Pearly Meg's," said Jack. "I've that job to do."

"Then you'll go by yourself."

"Whatever for?"

"There's snakes!"

"Give over."

"It's thrunk wi' 'em!"

"And who told you that?"

"Suit yourself."

"Nan Sarah, have you ever so much as seen one mortal snake there in all your born days?" said Jack.

"You don't have to see them. They see you. I'm not going in yon hole, not for love nor money."

"You can watch, then," said Jack.

The hills drew towards Bully Thrumble. It stood near the head of the valley, yet was its heart. The stone pillar, not the height of a big man, was the first and the last of the eye's every journey.

Jack and Nan Sarah walked together. Once the way in had begun, it was no time for speaking.

They crossed at the ford. Bully Thrumble looked above them on its bank.

"You go. I'll wait here."

"Come on with you." He took her hand and pulled her, stumbling, through the rushes, towards the trees.

"Jack! I'll get slutched!"

"You'll wash. There. Now what's here to be feart of?"

"Them trees."

The two thorn trees stood beside the brook, the only trees in Thursbitch. One of them was hung with cow chains and spancels, some still flecked bright, some rusted, but most webs of iron. On the other tree were ox yokes, horse shoes and collars. The yokes were

[29]

worm eaten, the collars old, their leather rotten and the straw fillings snagged in the branches.

"Jack. It's not the same, here. Them things. On the trees. And the nails."

"It'll not hurt. Now come on." He held her wrist and she had to follow him over the bog to Pearly Meg's. "You stand yonder and count snakes."

He bent under the flag roof and down between the close walls to the running water of the well. At the bottom step he took the stem of grass from his hatband and held it before him. He dismembered it into four pieces and dropped them separately, and with each of them he spoke. "One for Crom. One for crow. One for Jenkin. One for grow."

The water carried the ears into the hill. He raised his hat to the dark. "Thirsty work," he said, and crouched to dip the hat in the well.

"Jack! It's deadly poison!"

"So I've heard." He drank.

"Deadly poison!"

"But only the one day in the year."

"Do you not believe it?"

"I'll believe it. But I've found no wag yet as can tell me when that day is. It's not tonight, seemingly."

He grinned, put his hat on his head and went up the steps to Nan Sarah.

She picked a drier way through the rushes towards Bully Thrumble. He followed in the single track.

"Are you that bothered by snakes?"

"There's loads," said Nan Sarah. "Little stone dead uns in the brook. So where's the big uns if not in yon well?"

"I've not known anybody be hurt by owt here," said Jack; "just so long as it's done proper, and we mind us manners. It's what ways are for. Do you not agree?"

"I need to know as how you do," said Nan Sarah. "You're forever full of oddments in the mind when you've been over them hills. Every time the bells are gone, a part of me fears I'll not hear 'em again."

He put his arm around her shoulder and hugged.

"Nan Sarah. I may leave in the crook of the moon; but I'm back in its every wild waning."

They sat by Bully Thrumble and Jack took off her shawl.

"What's this hard?" he said.

"A dog turd, I shouldn't wonder."

He laughed and lay back on the grass. She lifted herself on one elbow, and her eyes grew gentle and stern as she lowered her face on his.

"Nan Sarah." He cupped the back of her head. "What makes you look so?"

She gave no answer.

"I've walked long," he said, "and I've been in many parts, and I've seen things and heard tales and sung songs; but this here nook of the world, for me, smiles more nor any other. And the way you looked at me then has made me fit to skrike. Nan Sarah."

She raised herself.

"Jack. I'm teeming."

"Is it me?"

"Of course it's you, you dimmock. You and maybe a bit of him."
She looked up at Bully Thrumble.

"What do you want to do?" said Jack. "Shove it under a stone?"

"It's what do you want, Jack?"

"You're definite it's me? None of them down Saltersford?"

"You, Jack."

"But you feel the same. You look the same. Thin as a rasher of wind."

"Oh, Jack. Be told. Now what do you want doing?"

"Has Ma Mary ketched on?"

"There's more nor nits in that one's head."

"What do you think?"

"Jack. Jack."

"Nan Sarah. You're all as I've ever needed in all this world. Did you not know?"

"You seem never suited. Forever agate. Like as you'll never rest."

"But that's my way," said Jack. "I'm a jagger born, me. I walk in my own shoon. And the more I see the more I want to be with you. Not some trollop else. And if you are teeming, and you'll keep it and take me, then I'll be a toad with two side pockets."

"Now it's me skriking," she said.

"I've to be in Chester, night after tomorrow, so I'm off first thing," he said. "And then there's a four-seam jag to be fetched at Northwich. But the day I get back we go up Thoon. So you see to it as all's ready."

"It's ready now," she said.

She felt inside her shawl.

"You fause monkey!" said Jack.

"'Better bad than bout'," said Nan Sarah.

"You were reckoning on it all along!"

She smiled.

"You'll do, Nan Sarah. You'll do."

She was holding the Blue John. Cheesecloth was tied over the top.

They left Bully Thrumble, crossed the brook and began the climb to Catstair. They held hands but did not speak. Thoon was the skyline of the ridge, and in their way was Biggening Brom. The stone stood on the moor side, as tall as Nan Sarah, its top weathered to a head and neck, its back straight and the belly nine months gone.

Nan Sarah undid the cheesecloth from the Blue John. Inside was a piece of honeycomb. She took it in her hand, and spread the honey over the top, and down and round until the stone shone in the lowering sun. Then she turned to face Jack.

With his knife he cut a button from his shirt and set the button on the honey. Next he cut a strip from the edge of his britches, and fixed it to the stone. He knelt on one knee and lifted the hem of Nan Sarah's skirt. She did not move. He cut the same length from her petticoat and laid it crossways on the other strip. He took her hand and placed hers and his on the belly of the stone. Then, the hands holding, they went on up the moor.

Catstair was long and steep, and steeper; but always Thoon waited.

They reached the square slab of the top and stood looking out across Thursbitch. The sun was sliding from Andrew's Edge into Redmoor.

"Set your foot there," said Jack. "No. T'other."

There was a shallow print in the rock, and Nan Sarah's shoe fitted. Jack spoke to the hills.

"I give up this button, and a bit of waistband of me own britches, and a taste of Nan Sarah's petticoat, and a comb of the bees, in remembrance and mark of as how we made this holy station; and may they rise in glory to prove it for us in our last days."

They looked at each other and drew the sweetness against the other's lip. Then they left the top and went to the mouth of Thoon.

Nan Sarah felt the arch of the cave, the stones of the back, the crevice, the bottom slab.

"Whoever can have made this?"

"Summat bigger nor us, wife. There's things up here. I can tell you. What! A man can see all sorts."

They sat inside Thoon. The rock took them and held them. The first of night moved down the sky and the land merged.

"I never thought as how there were so many hills," said Nan Sarah. "Jack, it fears me for you now."

"You need never fear for me, Nan Sarah. Here's where I was born, you daft woman. There's no hurt."

"Born here? Where?"

"On this very stone. At least, that's what's said. But I reckon it was some wench as couldn't thole, and the chap fetched it and left it. But it couldn't have been long. Me father told me. There was a great dumberdash, and it let against Shining Tor, above Longclough. Mark's there still, if you look. Anyroad, me father, he's leading his kyne up Thursbitch; and he sees this here thunderbolt hit the side of Tor; and didn't they run! So he's going to look, when he sees me lying in Thoon, snug as a bug in a rug. Leastways, that's what he says. But I've always reckoned as it was a bit too much chance, like. Have you not been up before?"

"All them hills. Why should I?" she said. "There's work for neither man nor beast in these parts."

"There's work for me," he said. "And for me beasts. There's not a brow nor a clough nor a slade nor a slack, nor a cop nor a crag, nor a frith nor a rake, nor a moss nor a moor, as we don't know it, by day and by night, for as far as you can see and further."

"Is there no end?" she said.

"Nobbut The Unvintaged Red Erythræan Sea. Same as they say."

"That big pond down there?"

"That's no pond, Nan Sarah. It looks like it now, I'll grant you. But you get down there and it's neither flat nor wet; and right t'other side's Chester. And that's a two-day jag and a whealy mile, I can tell you. And I'll be laying me head there night after next."

"You shall come back?"

"I shall come back. I'm the promise as always comes back."

"I never knew," she said.

"Well, you know now. A man wi' salt in his pocket always gets home."

"There's a star falling. See at it!"

"Following its road. Same as me."

7

"Sal. Please. Use the gate."

"I prefer the griddle cat."

She teetered over the steel bars.

"You'll fall."

"Shut up, Ian. I'm concentrating."

"Then hold on to something."

"I like the odds."

He closed the gate.

"Put your leg in bed." She linked arms with him, and they went down and up to Howlersknowl.

Beyond the farmhouse the track turned off and climbed aslant the field. To the side and below was a yellow boulder with a steel ring fixed into the top. The soil was bare around it and its sides were polished dark with the rubbing of sheep.

They passed on, up to the gateway of the valley mouth.

"You were right about the stones," he said. "This one doesn't look like a post, either. It's much too big. What else can it be?"

"I've no idea. Oh. The valley."

"Nothing's changed," he said. "Just as it was."

"Wrong. Everything's different."

"What do you mean, everything?"

"Over the winter it's moved about three point seven millimetres."

"You are absurd," he said.

"On the contrary. I'm approximately accurate."

She put her head on his shoulder.

"That's an interesting feature."

"What is?" he said.

"The outcrop on the ridge, to the left, with a track going up."

"Sal?"

"Yes?"

"Look. Look at it. Look at it closely."

"Why?"

"What do you know about it?"

"At this distance? It's an outcrop. Rough Rock or Chatsworth Grit, probably. At a pinch it could be Roaches or Carbor. Namurian, certainly. What's the matter?"

"Nothing."

"Yes there is."

"No. Really."

"Come on. Tell Mummy."

"It's nothing."

She held his arms, looked hard at him.

"I've done it again, haven't I?"

He did not answer.

"Yes. I have. I have. But what?"

"Let's go back."

"Ian."

"Come on."

"No. I mustn't hide. Mustn't dodge. I can't pretend. I must fight this thing. Tell me."

"We parked, and walked from Pym Chair," he said. "Remember?"

"Pym Chair?"

"Where they were flying their model planes."

"We did?"

"We walked along the ridge."

"And I don't like crowds."

He nodded.

"All those people."

"Yes."

"A rock."

"Yes."

"There was a rock."

"Yes."

"Hollow. We sat. It was good."

"Yes."

"And that's it."

"Yes."

"Oh, Jesus Christ."

"We can go somewhere else."

"No. Here. There's something here. For me."

She huddled on a remnant of wall, her back against the big stone, and looked inwardly along the valley. He sat next to her, holding each hand in his.

The air was only far sounds.

She slammed her head on the stone and howled, thrashing from side to side; then slumped forward, her face in their hands. He felt the heat of her tears and the water from her mouth run on his palms. He held, gentle, and did not speak as she retched. Then she was quiet, and he was still.

She lifted her head and looked again. Her face was put together. Her breathing grew calm. Soon she gave him a quick little smile.

"What's that house?"

"It's a farm. A ruin. Thursbitch."

"Thursbitch. Have we been there?"

"Yes."

"Thursbitch. Yes. All right."

The path dipped and rose as they crossed gullies running off Cats Tor and the ridge. Nearer the ruin the path cut deep through banks of purple shale.

"Is this coal?" he said.

"Almost. Aha. Just what you'd expect."

She picked something out of the shale and gave it to him.

"It's an ammonite," he said.

"No. *Reticulosus bilingue.*"

"Which two?"

"Which two what?"

"Languages?"

She laughed. He watched her.

"Oaf. It's one of the main horizon indicators. Different species are used to identify individual series. So hereabouts we're in R-Two Marsdenian country. It's only bloody jargon."

"Wait." He opened his bag and took out a notebook. "Marsdenian R-Two. That's what you said on the outcrop."

"Which goes to show how clever I am."

They were at the ruin.

"If you're lucky, I may find you some R. *superbilingue* in the brook. And don't you dare ask if it's polyglot!"

She walked around the ford, turning stones over and picking up shale in the bed.

"Here we are. Another present." She put the fossil into his hand.

"I can't see any difference," he said.

"And that, my lad, is why I'm me and you're you. Give or take. More or less."

He helped her up the bank. They sat on a fallen post, and he opened a Thermos flask and poured for them both.

"Cold?"

"No. Fine. Good coffee."

She looked around at the valley.

"Penny for them."

"Mm." She turned her head.

"More coffee?"

"Thanks. Oh, buggeration."

The cup slipped and rolled down the grass. He went to pick it up, filled it again, and she took it in both hands.

"What was the mm?" he said.

"Just an mm."

"No it wasn't. Tell me."

"If you don't see, you probably can't be told."

"Try me."

"You really haven't sussed?"

"Sussed what?"

She looked at him, smiled and put her mouth down to the coffee.

"You get places," she said. "Usually it's no big deal. This is."

"I'm not with you."

"It knows we're here."

"Sorry?"

"And we are being watched."

"Where?"

"In that outcrop."

He lifted his binoculars. "No one. Look."

"Pointless," she said. "I'm fingers and thumbs. But it does know."

"You're a scientist."

"Precisely."

8

He came in, carrying two pails of water on a yoke. He set them down on the brewis floor and went into the houseplace and lifted a bag from above the mantle beam.

"Has a man got to do everything himself?"

"I'll help," said Nan Sarah.

"No licking fingers, mind."

Jack put the bag on the slopstone and drew up the pig bench for them to sit on. Nan Sarah brought a small knife and Jack took his out and wiped it. He opened the bag and sniffed. Then he broke off a cap and nibbled, tasting, and spat it onto the slopstone.

"They'll do."

He emptied the bag and spread the toadstools so that he could turn each piece over.

"You take legs," he said, "and me heads. Cut 'em longroads, but don't cut 'em too thin, else they'll go to nowt. We don't want crumbs."

They divided the caps from the stems and Nan Sarah began to cut each dry stem lengthwise into four strips. Jack looked closely at every brown cap and cut them into six segments, missing the white warts where he could.

"Ma Mary?"

"What?"

"Fetch us me resounding Thesprotian kettle. It's in the stable."

"Where do you want it?" Mary came back with a three-legged iron pot, carrying it by its handle.

"On the slopstone."

She banged it down and went out to the yard.

Jack and Nan Sarah worked, dropping each piece into the kettle.

"I've been thinking," she said.

"Eh, then."

"No. I have. About what you said that time. Was it right?"

"Was what right, Nan Sarah?"

"As how your father found you, up Thoon."

"It's what he reckons."

"How old were you?"

"Me belly button had been tied, but it was still wet, he said."

"And he saw no one?"

"There's plenty rocks to hide a man."

"And you weren't clemmed nor starved?"

"Ah. Now there's a thing you don't ask him, Nan Sarah. He told me; but he won't speak to nobody else. And even me just the once. Mind you, I suppose he could have told me mother; but she never said. And she'll not now, will she, from where she's gone?"

"Shall you tell me?" said Nan Sarah.

"I can't speak for the truth of it. Richard Turner's been a father to me, and a good father and all. But this here put summat on him. I don't know what. He said as how, when he found me, like; he said me mouth was covered in bees. He thought they'd stung me to death. But, he said, they weren't stinging me. They were feeding me. Bees. Then, when they see him, they all fly away into that big crack aback of Thoon; same as it was a nest. That's what he said."

"And do you think it's right?"

"How can I know? But one thing's for sure. I've never had a sting from a bee in all my life. Wasps, yes. But never bees. It feels as if they know; somehow. But I'll tell you what. And this is summat I've never told no one else. I've always had this feeling. It's always in me head, at the back of me mind, as how there's two of me. Same as if I had another half. And it's to do wi' bees."

They went on with the cutting. Jack brushed the small bits from the slopstone into his hand, even the piece he had tasted, and put them in the kettle and wiped both the knives. He opened the door.

"Ma Mary?"

"What is it now?"

"Last year's bilberries. Where are they?"

"Hanging in the shippon. Are you too idle to get 'em? Because I can't reach."

"Oh, thee hoe thy taters," said Jack.

He held a linen bag, blotched purple.

"They've lasted well," he said. "Neither wet nor dry."

He put the mouth of the bag into the pot and tipped the berries in. Then he took one of the pails and poured the water over. The other pail he set aside. "See as yon's not touched, agen we need a drop more."

"It's just water, Jack."

"You know better, Nan Sarah. That water's been fetched."

"Where do you get it?"

"Aback o' beyond. That's where. Aback o' beyond."

"Why won't the brook do?"

"Brook water boils. This never will. And that's what we must have."

He stirred the pot with a twig, then put it to hang over the fire and went on stirring.

"How is it you as knows all this nominy?" said Nan Sarah.

"Eh dear. Questions. Questions."

"Jack."

"Truth is, wife, I was lifted up. Same as at this Jenkin coming. Yet we always seem to thole it, somehow, for the next eighteen year odd. In between, each year's a recollecting. Recollecting promise. This year it'll be the whole beggaring cheese."

"Last Jenkin," she said, "I was that little. It was all racket and I couldn't see."

"I could," said Jack.

"What happened?"

"We were lifted up."

He stirred the blue red liquid.

"Why is it you?"

"I was lifted up. There's always someone as knows corbel bread and bilberries and piddlejuice; and the rest of that caper. I reckon as how there must be a great ruck of sense we'll never plunder. It's no use getting mithered. A man can't do nowt about it. There. That's near as ninepence."

He lifted the kettle from its hook and dropped the twig in the fire.

"Let it stand a seven-night, and we'll be ready. We shall that. We shall and all. Thesprotian."

9

"Well, well, well; so you're for off, I see," said Mary.

"Buckets for wells, Ma Mary," said Jack. "Ay. The night is the night, if the man is the man. But there's work to be done first." He tied a neckcloth, red with white spots. "I'll be back this after." He took a stem out of the kettle and swallowed it, washing it down with a mouthful of the liquid. And another. "Time to see if Old Bouchert's fit." He picked up his stick and a sack, and left the brewis.

The wind was light from the east, so he went up by Redmoor and along the side of Andrew's Edge to Sprout-kale Jacob. Nothing was moving in Thursbitch.

He went down the slope to Bully Thrumble, walking quietly. He sat with his back against the pillar, on the other side from the water, and listened. The sound of the brook entered him, and he grew to the stone. He waited. The sun was singing, but not loudly, and the small white clouds rang against each other, soft as Jinney's bells.

He plucked two wide blades of grass and held them between his thumb joints and blew. They cried out. He blew again. Lying flat, he peered round the base of the stone. Nothing. He wriggled back, and this time blew a harsher note; then looked again.

Downstream and across the ford, a white hare had risen from its form and was listening. It sank down, but he marked where it sat. He pulled back and stood with Bully Thrumble between them and took off his neckcloth. The wind was blowing across his scent. He laid the sack and the hat and the stick on the ground and moved to the front of the stone, letting no light between, holding the cloth in front, and walked slow and steady towards the form.

He crossed the water, making no sound. The land did not fail. There was a thistle stem. He came to it and draped the neckcloth over, and again was still. The hare did not run.

Jack walked backwards, and the land and the water held him, each foot set down in line with the other. Bully Thrumble met him and he turned around it. On the other side, he lay and looked. The neckcloth nodded in the wind.

Jack crawled on his belly through the reeds, away by a hillock and down to a bend in the brook towards Pearly Meg's. He crossed the brook, and used the cover of a gully to crouch up the other side as far as Biggening Brom.

From Biggening Brom he crawled until the red and white of the neckcloth was in line with Bully Thrumble. He rose in a clean move, and stood. The song of the sun and the chiming clouds covered all noise, and the wind was still cross-scented. He went on down.

The hare sat in its form, watching the sway of the red and white flower on its stem. Jack slid one hand under the body from behind and with the other flattened the ears back; and he was but a part of the hill that took the hare and lifted it against his chest. "Good day to you, Sir. I bless you with my elbow," he said.

He stroked the ears and spoke softly as he took the neckcloth and walked down to the ford and up to Bully Thrumble. "Old Bouchert. Old Turpin. Old Wimount. Old Goibert."

At Bully Thrumble he lowered himself and nestled the hare in the crown of his hat, talking and stroking, until he and the hare and the brook and the valley were one, below Thoon. He lifted his hand, and the hare slept.

Now Jack stood with his stick and the sack, and the reeds caressed him and the marsh did not hold him and he took the way to Pearly Meg's.

He bent under the roof and down the steps.

At the bottom, he listened to what the water told him, and then tapped the stones lightly; and from the cracks between, the snakes came and curled themselves round the twists of his stick, and when they were all counted and quiet he laid the stick below the roof and reached into the hill. With both hands he felt in the dark for the shelf over which the water ran, and took the weight that sat there, holding its wetness to him until he was free to turn and put it into the sack.

He went to the light and Bully Thrumble. He lifted his hat and nestled it in his arm, slung the sack over his shoulder, and set off, black stooped, down to Saltersford.

10

They were gathered around Jenkin: Lathams, Adsheads, Potts, Ridges, Lomases, Slacks, Oakeses, Swindells, Turners, Martha Barber; excited, still, and nervous; looking to the sky and where the lane cut a notch in the hill at Pym Chair.

Jack Turner had set the iron kettle on the ground and put the sack against the pillar of Jenkin. He waited for the last to arrive, straggling along the seven ways. The hare was quiet on his elbow, hidden in the red and white neckcloth. Richard Turner stood by him and watched.

"You'll master him, do you think?"

"Nay, not master, Father," said Jack. "Thole is best I can hope for."

"Last time, he took John Pott. And John Pott was three days a-dying."

"But he wouldn't be so sharp by then, would he?" said Jack. "He'd done it twice. Not so quick."

"He was turning sixty; and that with a tail."

"There you are," said Jack. "And it had been Potts for a good while, hadn't it? Maybe it's not but right to pass it on, so as young uns can learn, and it's not lost."

"I don't know," said Richard Turner. "But it was you he put it to. His last words to me were, 'See as Jack's reared, agen next time'. And you can't nay a man when he's dying."

"I never knew."

"I never told."

Jack stroked the hare and looked into its eyes.

"Buckets for wells, Father."

He stroked the hare and laid the folded neckcloth on the ground. "Right, then," he said. "Is all here as is coming? Let's be having you."

He opened the mouth of the sack and peeled it down. There were mutterings, and some gasps of love. He took the stone head and raised it for them to see. He stretched, and set it on the top of Jenkin, so that the head and the pillar were one being. Richard Turner handed him a wooden cup and Jack dipped it into the kettle.

"Here's first to Crom."

He dribbled the blue red juice over the head. It ran into the staring all-seeing blind eyes and down over white Jenkin.

"Next to his Bester."

He reached inside the cloth and marked the hare with his finger in a line along the nose and between the ears.

The people formed up and Jack dipped the cup full for each and gave a piece of cap or stem. After they drank, they sat at the lane side, waiting.

"Not you, Nan Sarah." He spoke under his breath.

"Why not?" she said. "See. I've fetched Blue John special."

"You don't sup when you're carrying. You could lose it."

"A wet of me lips, then."

He looked at the sky. The sun had set behind Pike Low.

"A taste, and no more."

He took the Blue John and dampened the rim and gave it back to her. She licked the trace, pretended to drink, smiled and put the Blue John in her shawl, and went to sit with the others.

"Don't you leave yourself short," said Richard Turner.

"There's far and plenty, Father. I've thought on that."

He was the last to drink. He wiped the cup dry with his finger, swallowed what was uneaten, and lifted the kettle and drained it. Then he took up the covered hare and sat on the bank.

They waited.

"Ri-chooral!" sang Tally Ridge.

No one spoke or moved, but watched.

Tally Ridge stood and began to dance.

"Ri-chooral! Ri-addiday!" His step was broken, but he did not stagger, and he moved his arms around with his shoulders, graceful, yet to no rhythm or pattern. "Ri-chooral! Ri-chooral! Ri-chooral! I-day!" He sat. His head was dipping and twisting with the same movement, and his mouth made nearly a grin. Then he fell over, asleep.

They waited.

"Ta-ba-li!" sang Jane Thomas. But she did not move.

Jack watched them and the sky. He smoothed the hare's ears.

"Ku-kur!"

"Ukush-li-li-gi!"

The cries broke out on every side, and many people began to dance, alone and together, but all moved in the smooth way of snakes.

"Jack, I'm frit."

"No need, wife. Sit close by the bank. There's no harm in them. They'll not hurt you."

"Ta-ba-ri-gi!"

"Sithee!" On the cut of the hill the moon's rim showed. Tally Ridge was awake. "Goibert in Pym Chair!"

Jack lifted the head from Jenkin. He pulled the sack over it, hoisted it on his shoulder and made his way back along the lane towards Saltersford. The hare rested on his arm.

He lost the moon as the lane dipped. From Saltersford he climbed between the avenue of the high stones, close against the hill. He felt the throb of the ground as he had before and measured it with every stride.

"Walk and do. Walk and do. Walk and do till all is done."

He crossed the Butts, the Belderstone near the track and the steel ring glinting from it, up by Lankin into Thursbitch. He did not hurry.

"Walk and do. Walk and do. Walk and do till all is done. Walk and do. Walk and do. Walk and do till all is done."

He crossed the ford and sat by Bully Thrumble, facing Thoon, now a stark rock. He breathed the night flowers of the valley. The hare was calm, but a tear formed in each glowing eye.

"Old Bouchert. Old Bouchert. Not long now. Not long at all. Sithee."

Light limned the rock of Thoon, and the disk seemed to be born from the cave itself.

"Sithee, sithee, little lad. Why, look ye. There's your ears, and your pretty head."

He rose.

"And the night is the night."

He passed over the water that was already shining and began the climb up Catstair.

"Walk and do. Walk and do. Walk and do till all is done."

By the time he reached the cave the moon was well up, with the shape of a hare clear across its face.

Jack took the head of Crom and set it on the floor of the cave, looking out across the valley.

"I'll be back in a three-night," he whispered into the stone ear. "Give us thy bonny een now, then sleep gen tha be weary."

He left the head to watch over its land and stepped onto the square slab under the ridge of the moor.

The moon was bright, but a low mist lay across the ground. He opened his neckcloth and the hare stood up. It looked about and around, sniffing the air, then lolloped away into the mist.

Jack sat, one heel beneath him, and waited. The night was still. He watched. Listened. Waited. He tucked his neckcloth into his shirt. And waited. The moon rose higher, drawing with it the mist. Jack stood to see above it, listening, looking on the hare's path.

The first stars were showing, their sounds the echoes of the moon, and the moonlight on the brook rippled up to him. As in the day, he took of the valley and the sky and the valley and the sky took of him; but now all was lapped in a greater silence, and in it and from it he heard something in front of him, and a rustling and a plashing in the mist.

Jack stood firm and waited. The rustling and the plashing drew near, the mist snorted, and of it and from it came a bull, a great white bull, marked only by a red stripe along its muzzle, dark in the moon.

"O sweet Bull. O noble Bull. O worthy Bull. O bonny Bull."

11

Nan Sarah sat on the bank side. Everyone else was asleep. They lay in the lane or were propped against stones and each other, silent, but with their limbs moving in a slowness of their own. The moon was clear of Cats Tor.

Clonter Oakes lifted his head and looked around. He caught hold of Mary Turner's skirt to pull himself onto his knees, and she woke at the feel of him. He stood, swaying but in balance, and not drunk, lifted his arms and clicked his fingers. He danced. His feet barely left the ground, but moved across, heel and toe, a pattering weave of steps.

Others woke at the sound and danced too. Once they were up they were firm and their bodies flowed. They danced where they stood, the men matching but not watching Clonter. The women had a different way: three high steps and a hop; and as they hopped, they wrenched their heads back over their shoulders. They lifted their arms and brought them down, the elbows bent.

Nan Sarah did not know what to do. Without pausing or speaking, the dancers formed, the men on the outside, and they came together with their different steps into one dance. The women leapt higher and the men danced faster. At no signal, they started off down to Saltersford, each one spinning slowly around.

Richard Turner sang. After two lines of the song, Edward Turner sang two lines, alone. The next two they sang together. Then all the people sang.

Nan Sarah followed, apart, walking. She did not know the dance and she did not know the words.

Sneaper Slack began a second verse, and Tally Ridge took over.

Nan Sarah had to walk hard to keep up with them. For all their sound and force, they did not tire.

Lither Lomas sang:

> "The third great joy of Mary Anne
>> It were the joy of three — "

Fodder Pott sang:

> "To see her own son little Jack
>> Upon the horn to fly."

Their voices joined:

> "Upon the horn to fly and scrat
>> The moon as bright as day."

Saltersford echoed:

> "Euoi! Euoi! Io! Euoi!
>> Through all Eternity!"

Another round began.

> "The next great joy of Mary Anne
>> It were the joy of four — "

> "To see her own son little Jack
>> March down into the moor."

> "March down into the moor and draw
>> The well as none can dry."

> "Euoi! Euoi! Io! Euoi!
>> Through all Eternity!"

They danced up the hill between the high stones.

> "The next great joy of Mary Anne
>> It were the joy of five — "

> "To see her own son little Jack
>> Fetch out the head alive."

"Fetch out the head alive and skrike
　　　He were the same as he."
"Euoi! Euoi! Io! Euoi!
　　　Through all Eternity!"

The climb to Shady did not slow them. Their voices were no less.
On and on. When they came to the end of the song, they sang again.
Over and over. Nan Sarah fell behind.

"The next great joy of Mary Anne
　　　It were the joy of six – "
"To see her own son little Jack
　　　Call from the rock the snakes."
"Call from the rock the snakes and shape
　　　Of them the ivy tree."
"Euoi! Euoi! Io! Euoi!
　　　Through all Eternity!"

When they reached the Butts, they did not go into the field, but
stood at the corner and were stilled. Nan Sarah came up with them.
They took no notice of her, nor of each other, but all looked towards
the mouth of Thursbitch. They waited.

The Belderstone was dark on the field, but the crescent ring set into
the top took a greater light, gathering the moon.

They waited.

12

"O bonny Bull. Come thy ways."

He stroked the curls of the bull between its horns. Then he turned his back. The moon was on the ford and all the waters of the valley ran silver to it; the high stones shone.

He set off down Catstair. He took a bone pipe from his pocket and began to play. The tune was happy and sad, and the night flowers opened and swayed around and below him, and he could see every one as close as if he held it; while around and above him the stars were just as close and moved with the flowers; and all rang and sang with the brook to the tune; and under was the knell of the tread of the bull.

They came down Catstair to the ford and along the valley. Thursbitch waters purled on every side. The flowers were with the stars, the stars were flowers, and the brook was the Milk Path all the way to Lankin at the end of the valley. Beyond, the hills were in moonlight. Jack put the pipe in his pocket. The flowers closed. The stars held their roads. He stood and looked down to the Butts. All that shone was the glint of the steel ring in the Belderstone. The people were dark and silent across the field.

The bull came to Jack's side, and he laid his arm along its neck. "Noble Bull. Worthy Bull. We live each other's life and die each other's death."

He walked into the field, his arm still on the bull, to the Belderstone. A rope lay coiled upon it, with other things. At the stone, he pressed the neck and the bull knelt.

"We do not want to mither you, O Moon," he said, "with worship or ill praise, pasturing in your heart swift eyeless love."

He lifted the rope and wound it between the horns. He measured five paces of slack and tied the free end to the ring in the stone; and spoke.

"Shine with high light, O Bull, and sharpen your two horns, while you sleep below the sky now in these white nights. Let your bonny een give new een above at harvest end, and let your voice go belder to the Moon, so as he never sets for ever, but wakens to tragwallet on his ways, for all us sakes."

He called aloud.

"See at white Bull! Bonny Bull! As lives on hill tops; striding Bull as lives on hill tops! Lord over all as close the eye!"

The people sang. "Io!"

"See at his step, full of honey! There in his highmost step, the honey!"

"Io!"

"There the highmost step of Bull, striding the sky, shines down! For there is nowt as he is not!"

"Io! Euoi!"

"See at Bull with mighty voice! Mask of Bull, kindled for beauty, white!"

He lifted two wooden pegs and drove them into the sockets of the eyes, and thrust pepper with his fist down the throat as it opened to roar.

The people ran. They fell upon the bull with their strength, tearing, baying, gnawing, as the bull flailed, held by the rope, five paces from the stone.

Jack sprang onto its neck and gripped the horns.

"The Bull I sing!
And for ever yon Bull shall last!"

~~~~~~~~~

Fodder Pott was lofted into the air, and leapt back, hanging under the throat.

> "First song from the kettle, when was it spoken?
>   Is it not the kettle of the Moon's heat?"

The screaming women laughed and never lost hold.

> "We know not on what day the Bull arose!
> We know not on what day, nor what was the cause!
> Nor on what hour of that day the Moon was born,
> Him as is first to die and first to be again!
> Come! Come! Ne'er mind thy shape nor name,
> O Bull! O mountain Bull! Snake of a hundred heads!
> Flame! Beast! Wonderment! Come!"

The nails and teeth had pierced the hide. The men and women tore, ate, and the guts flew in the dance and the song.

The bull dropped. Jack ripped out the heart.

"Now have you died and now are born, twice happy Bull, in this one night."

13

Nan Sarah could not see what was happening. Her back ached. She sat against a high stone, and above her were the shapes of the silent people facing Thursbitch and the risen moon.

She heard Jack's voice up the field, talking at first, as if there was someone with him. The people rustled and jostled but made no other noise. Then Jack shouted, but what it was she could not hear. The people answered. Jack's voice again. And then the people's. Nan Sarah stood, but could not see past the height of the men. Jack called to them, and they called back more loudly still.

Jack called, but his voice sang, and the people surged forward up the field, so fast that Nan Sarah had to stop and watch them close upon the Belderstone.

Against the moonlight she could not make out the shapes. They were one swarm of noise. She heard Jack again, but his was the only mortal voice, and even for him Nan Sarah could not move. Something was in the field. It grew from the mass, and was it, yet made it more, drawing the dark writhing into its own purpose, the yelling to its own tongue. What was there grew to reach the moon and gave one cry such as Nan Sarah had not heard in all her days: the cry of both man and bull.

Then it fell apart and came towards her down the hill, turning back to those she knew: Oakeses, Swindells, Turners, Potts, Adsheads, Lomases, Slacks, Lathams, Ridges, all running, dancing, but alone, knowing of nothing but what they themselves had done and seen.

"Jack! Where's Jack?"

No one stopped. They laughed. They sang. She saw their clothes streaming tattered. "Where's Jack?" She tried to hold them, but their limbs slipped through her fingers in grease, and her hands became too wet to grip. She saw lame Martha Barber springing high. "Where's Jack?" Martha answered, but gagged upon her speech. Then they were gone, down to Saltersford, and Nan Sarah was alone on the Butts, in the silence, beneath the moon, before the yellow stone.

"Jack!"

Nothing answered. She went to the stone.

He lay beside it. His clothes were torn, and he had been bitten and clawed. Even in the moonlight she saw the blood coming from his mouth and swollen eyes. She tried to clean him with her shawl, using the dew. He breathed, but the breath was slow and harsh. She kissed him, and he groaned. He coughed, but it was indrawn.

She pushed her fingers between his lips. A tooth fell back in his throat, lodged against his tongue and she caught it. Then she put his head between her knees and forced the jaw so that she could hook the tongue up and forward. He groaned again, but his breathing was stronger though still harsh.

"Jack. Jack, love."

He lifted his hand. She took it, but he pulled it clear and blindly felt for her shawl.

He tried to speak.

"Graa. Graa."

"What?"

"Graa." His fingers moved along her shawl. "Graa." He felt the Blue John.

"Graa."

His hand was urgent, and she took out the cup. But he did not try to hold it. He pointed to the flap of his britches.

"Graa. Graa. Graa."

Then to his lips.

"What, Jack?"

He pulled at the flap, but could not unlace it. She did it for him. His hand felt around for the cup. She gave it to him, but it slipped and he could not grasp. He pointed down again.

"Graa."

She held it for him and he filled it. Then he pointed to his lips again and opened his mouth. She lifted the cup. The smell was sweet and fragrant, nectar. She poured drops onto his tongue and he swallowed, then opened his mouth again. She went on till he had emptied the cup. Nan Sarah dabbed his mouth with her shawl.

"Grallus."

His head fell sideways. She smelled his breathing, cradled him and sat while he slept.

He slept until the moon had set, and day broke.

Dew covered them both.

He moved, and lifted his head and spat. Nan Sarah kissed his brow. He opened one eye as much as he could.

"Now then, love," he said.

"Jack. Whatever did they do at you?"

"By. Yon piddlejuice works wonders. Oh, me neck."

"Jack. What did they do?"

"Them? Nowt." He coughed. "Was it right? Was it seen right by? Did we mind us manners?"

"Jack, you've been half killed! They were for murdering you!"

"Never. Not them. Was Bull we served."

"What bull?"

"Summat on me chest." He went into a spasm of coughing, blood at first, then with one heave he stopped. He felt inside his mouth and dragged something from his throat.

He held a stained, matted lump of coarse white hair.

"Wife. We did it by right ways."

14

"You put your right arm in!
You put your right arm out!
In, out, in, out,
Shake it all about!
You do the Okey Kokey
And you turn around;
And that's what it's all about!
Yeh!
Oh, Okey Kokey Kokey!
Oh, Okey Kokey Kokey!
Oh, Okey Kokey Kokey!
Knees bend, arms stretch,
Ra, ra, ra!"

They bowled along Pike Low, swinging together as they sang. The windows were open.

"You put your right leg in!
You put your right leg out!"

"Mind the gears!"

"In, out, in, out,
Shake it all about!"

At the brow of Pike Low the hills leapt up.

"Open the roof, Ian! We need more room!"

As they curved down towards Blue Boar, he folded the roof back with one hand.

"You put both legs in!
  You put both legs out!"
She waved her feet in the air, her hands above her head.
"And that's what it's all about!
  Yeh!"
From Blue Boar up Ewrin Lane to Waggonshaw Brow.
"You put your whole self in!
  You put your whole self out!"
"Sit down! Fasten your seat belt!"
"Seat belt! Sit down!
  Ra, ra, ra!"
He slowed and stopped at Buxter Stoops. They could not see for the
tears. She slipped as far down onto the floor as the seat would let her,
and pulled at the grab handle and the steering wheel to get herself
up. His head was resting on the wheel, tears of laughter running down
his cheeks, and when the wheel turned he fell across her lap. They lay
until he could sit straight. His neck bounced on the headrest. He took
a handful of tissues and passed the box to her. They mopped and
wiped and spluttered. At last they had control to stay upright. They
turned to each other, red eyed, gasping.

He closed the roof, and then the windows. "I'm not switching this
engine on, woman, until you behave yourself. From here, I need my
wits, without your bawling demotic rubbish in my ear."

"Yes, Ian," she said, and stuffed tissues into her mouth.

He drove down the steep-banked lane. There was no place for
two cars to pass. He was in second gear all the time to the three-
way junction and beyond, turning left round Nab End into
Saltersford.

The land was as level as it could be, for the valley. Then they went
past Jenkin Chapel and up towards Pym Chair. At Howlersknowl he
left the road and vibrated across the cattle grid.

"What are you doing?" she said.

"Conservation of mass and energy." The road dipped down and then up to the farmhouse. "I shan't be long."

He went to the door and knocked. The door opened and he spoke for a few moments. Then came back.

"OK. We can park here. Out you get."

He unlocked the boot.

"Oh no," she said. "No."

"Yes, Sal."

"No. Not those poncy sticks. I won't. I will not."

"They make a difference. I've tried them."

"I am not going to," she said. "I don't want to become one of these yomping urban oiks who don't know what they're doing or where they are. Good God. You'll have me in a Day-Glo jacket, next."

"Do I detect a hint of hubris?"

"You can detect what you sodding well like."

He took her hand to go through the yard to the hillside.

"Put those sticks back in the car, Ian."

"I may use them myself," he said.

"Ian?"

"Yes, Sal."

"You know just how many kinds of bastard you are, don't you?"

"People tell me often enough. But I don't let myself get on tender-hooks about it. Now are we going, or aren't we?"

They walked along the track between a stone wall and the farm garden.

"Ian?"

"What?"

"I'm sorry. The moods are the worst part."

"I know, Sal. I know."

They began the climb across the last field before the valley. She held his arm, but soon she could not control her stumbling. He said nothing, and they went on at her pace.

"Oh, damn, damn, damn, damn, damn. I really am sorry. Not a good day today. I've got to sit down."

"Over here," he said, and he took her to a yellow boulder and they both sat on it. "No rush. Take it easy."

She put her back against his.

"And that's what it's all about," she said at last.

He said nothing.

"You win. Show me how to use those footling sticks."

"Winning doesn't come into it." He adjusted the length of the trekking poles.

"Stand up. Now put your hand through the thong and grip the moulded piece."

"You know I don't have a grip," she said.

"Put your hand round, and your weight will do the holding. The poles are spring loaded. Now the other. To all intents and purposes, they give you two more legs. How's it feel?"

"As if I'm an over-articulated chimpanzee."

"I'd settle for over articulate," he said.

"Now what?"

"Just walk. But left pole with opposite right leg. The spikes will hold you and the rubber disks will stop you from sinking in. There'll be less lateral stress, too. Start by climbing, first. Back to the track."

She jabbed both poles into the grass and stood for a while, testing her balance. She took a cautious step. Then another.

"Try a normal stride," he said.

She moved, but the left pole went with the left foot, the right with the right. She fell sideways. He went to pick her up.

She was laughing too much to speak.

He lifted her under the arms and put her back on her feet. She began to shift her weight, but was overcome by giggling and rested her head on her hands on the poles.

She pushed her tongue forward inside her lower lip, jutted the jaw, furrowed her brow and set off, keeping time and measuring her strides with loud monkey grunts. When she reached the track, she turned and jangled her hands above her head, gibbering, pursing her lips. Then she strode off past the stone gateway into the valley.

"Wait for me!" He ran to catch up.

"This is great," she said. "Fan. Tastic."

They moved at a steady pace.

"Fan. Tastic. I'd forgotten what walking is."

"Careful going down. The balance shifts."

"Ian. It feels as though . . ."

She stopped and looked up and around.

"As though?"

"As though there's no difference."

"Between what?"

"Anything. There's no difference. I can't tell which is the valley and which is me."

"I can," he said. "My feet are my feet. And that water we've gone through is that water. Water does not have feet."

"What's the difference between your feet and the water?"

"My feet are dry. Water is wet."

"Wiggle your toes."

"So?"

"You are wiggling the valley and the valley is wiggling you. Third Law of Motion."

"Then what's this stile?"

She looked at it.

"I'll help you over," he said.

"No. But get ready to catch."

She shoved the poles into the mud and put one foot on the step. She pushed and leaned forward, so that when she toppled, the momentum brought the other foot up and she caught her balance by holding the side with one hand and using the friction of her body against the post to slow her movement. Then she lifted a pole, lodged it onto the step on the other side of the bar, and crossed over with the opposite foot. She brought the rear leg up behind her, but she could not bend it enough to clear the bar. She had to put it back down, and stood with one foot on either side.

"I'm stuck."

"Do it again; and I'll guide your leg."

"No."

She swung the other pole across and set the two together, holding them with one hand. She wrapped her forearm around the post and carried her weight forward, dropping her shoulders so that her hip raised the leg. The foot lay sideways on the bar.

"Let me help."

"No."

She moved to drag the foot free, and it snatched clear so quickly that she lost her balance and fell. She deflected herself from the rocky ground with one pole and slid down the stone wall.

"I'm OK."

"And what of the valley?" he said.

"It's establishing an intimate osmotic relationship with my arse."

By the time he had climbed over the stile she was on her feet and the poles again.

When they came to the ruin they stopped to rest and eat.

"Mind if I mooch around a bit?" he said.

"Help yourself. I shan't run far."

He wandered about the building and the ford, and then up the western slope. He stopped often to look at the ground. He was not gone long.

"So? What have you found?"

"Too many stone posts," he said. "I can't make sense of them. Most of them don't relate to any of the walls. A lot are just lying, as if they've been pulled up. I've measured some; and though they're different shapes, they're all about three point five cubic metres. And if the one standing above the ford is set in as far as they were, it'll be the same. How's that in weight?"

"About point seven of a tonne each," she said. "Probably the maximum practical load. They're getting to you, aren't they? It's this farmhouse that bothers me. The stones belong, but the house doesn't. What's here is a lot older."

"I can't cope with geological time scales," he said.

"Nobody can. What I'm talking about is to do with us."

"Another part of the mm factor?"

"The what?"

"Last time we were here you mentioned an mm."

"Did I? Yes. I suppose so. That would describe it. Let's walk. I want to have a look at that outcrop on the ridge up there."

"Which?"

"There's only the one," she said. "It's interesting."

They left the ruin and crossed the green field. At the top of the field a low, broken wall separated the pasture from the steep rough beyond.

"Head for the track we came down," he said.

"Came down?"

"Head for that brown track to the ridge. It goes past the outcrop."

They were nearly at the wild moor. Sheep scattered.

"There's another stone," he said. "How are you doing?"

"We'll get to it on the next traverse."

When they reached the stone, she rested on her poles. "Extraordinary. Nature improving on art."

"Is it?" he said. "It looks sculpted to me."

"It's natural erosion. There isn't a mark on it."

The stone was the figure of a heavily pregnant woman; peaked head; a straight neck running to a straight back down into the ground; a massive, rounded belly.

"Why build it into a wall?" he said.

"That may be your answer."

"What may?"

"Perhaps the wall was built to it."

"These walls are old."

"They are."

"That would imply that this is older."

"You always were the bright one, Ian."

"You're sure it hasn't been shaped?"

"Only by the wind. I'm not saying it wasn't chosen."

"And brought up here? Why? When?"

"I'm just a simple geologist."

He looked back across the valley.

"Yes," she said. "I'd guess about point seven of a tonne, like the others."

She settled on a piece of wall and ran her hands over the gritstone. He did the same, putting his on hers.

"It's beautiful."

"But what is the context?" he said.

"I'm sure you'll come up with one," she said. "For a start, it makes sense of the stone by the ford. If this is Effect, then the other's well equipped to be Cause. Let's sit and be quiet, shall we?"

"Wake up."

"What?"

"You've been asleep for twenty minutes."

"Have I? Ouch. Creeping crud. I'll believe you."

Still with one hand on the stone, she looked to the ridge.

"I think my eyes were bigger than this one's stomach. If we're to get back to the car, we'd better save the top for another day." She levered herself up. "The muscles are feeling it. And this is enough to remember."

She turned away from the stone and the ford and began towards the track out of the valley. "You were right. Definitely. Down is tough."

She moved more slowly, even when they were off the hill.

"Sorry. I've got to rest again. No need to sit. And you may find me less willful at the stile. Old age, you know. It comes to us all. Well, most of us. Mind where you're standing."

He looked down. "Oh, good grief," he whispered. He scanned the valley, took out his binoculars. "Don't talk. Keep moving. You must keep moving. To the stile. Come on. Now."

"Why?"

"This is marked as a public right of way. But some idiot. Sal. Move. We could be killed."

"Bullshit."

"Not funny. It's still warm."

He part carried, part dragged her, ignoring her pain, along the empty valley with its hidden folds, until they reached the stile. He picked her up and dropped her on the other side.

15

Jack lay on the settle as he had for the past three nights. Mary put cold compresses on his face and replaced them, and spooned water between his lips.

"Is sun up?" he said.

"Well up."

"How's day?"

"Mizzling."

"I must go get him home."

He swung his feet to the floor and pulled off the compresses.

"You're not taking no one nowhere," said Mary. "Not with that face. You favour a rotten mawkin."

"Give us me bag, Ma Mary."

"I will not," she said. "You lie down."

Jack stood and found the wall with his hands and worked his way to the door. He took his satchel from its peg and went back to the settle. He opened the satchel and felt around inside and brought out a wooden tube with a lid on one end. He lifted off the lid and shook three dried toadstools onto his palm. The stems were pale and the caps brown blotched white.

"Fetch us a jug of water," he said and pushed the three pieces between his split lips and began to chew. "Haste, woman."

Mary brought a jug. He put out his hands and she fitted them round. He lodged his upper teeth over the rim, tipped his head back and swallowed. He felt for the table, set the jug on it, then lay back on the settle and was quiet. Soon he slept.

Mary looked at the tube, without touching. She had seen it before, but never so near. Jack had always kept it covered. The tube was old and there were patterns carved on it: stars, dots, diamonds, crossed lines; a tree with some leaves on lopped branches between a hare and an animal with a long neck. On the other side was a cup or dish, and in it the stump of a tree with three sprigs; or, the other way up, it was a toadstool on its one leg.

Mary sat with Jack while he slept. He slept peacefully, the only movements were slight twitches of his limbs, which became a smooth rippling. She looked inside the tube, making no noise. It was packed with dried toadstools. She shook her head.

"Buckets for wells again, Ma Mary?"

Jack still lay on his side, his face blank with swelling, his mouth a purple cushion between moustache and beard, his nose a smear, his eyes bulged, marked only by the inward lashes of the turn.

He sat up and put the cap on the tube and the tube in the satchel, without pause or fumble.

"Jack. You can never see."

"A man must see to do a job, mustn't he?" He stood, put on his coat and hat, slung the satchel on his shoulder and opened the door. The fine rain was drifting, hiding the slopes in cloud. "Crom's dew," he said. "You'll have good harvest." He picked up the sack, a pat of butter and the remaining water pail from the brewis, and set off.

When he came to the Butts, he paused and listened. He moved forward and sat on the Belderstone and listened again. "Sup, me lads. Sup, me wenches." The air of Thursbitch was still and full of bright cloud. He heard the brook. And behind the brook, near and far in the valley, a noise, the same noise wherever it was, faint or loud, the sound of a drum in the earth, each a slow march for the water.

He went up to the corner and beyond to Lankin. Lankin was not

there; only the socket, and beyond, down the slope, a dent and flattened reed, and another further off; and from all Thursbitch the thump
of a tread in the ground.

Jack left the track and climbed straight for Cats Tor.

When he came near the line from the Broster Rocks he stopped
and listened again before moving. He saw the dents, and crossed over.

He changed direction and struck along the tor up to the level ridge
and to Thoon. The stone head in the cave looked out to the rain and
the cloud. He sat next to it and stroked its carved cheeks.

"Now then, old Crom. How hast tha been this journey? Did the
light hurt thine een? Never fret. It's done; while next time. We shall
burn bonny fires for thee. And Jenkin shall hold stars right running."
He felt his own lids and the stone. "Eh dear. We must look a pair, you
and me. But did you see at all your land and did we mind us ways?
I'll take you down and put you in your bed, as soon as stones have
done supping at the brook. We don't want to be trod on by them
great lummoxes. Hush now." He listened to the valley. The sound of
the earth had stopped. "Come up, old youth. They've done."

He pulled the sack over the head. He slung it over his shoulder,
took up the pail and began the way down Catstair. He paused at
Biggening Brom. She was firm in her reeds. He went to cross the ford.
Bully Thrumble stood above him, and the other stones around. There
were dents in the shale and mud everywhere about the ford.

He followed the brook to Pearly Meg's. First he lowered the sack
to the ground and took the pail down the steps and poured the unused
water back to the well. Then he brought the head, leaving the sack
outside, and set it back on its shelf. "Here's butter for thee." He reached
for his stick. The snakes were still coiled around it, but when he tapped
with his finger they left and went back into the rock.

Jack lifted his hat to the darkness.

"Peace to you, Crom, and blessing to you, Crom, and sleep to you,

Crom; and may the heat of the Moon be ever on you and on us all."

He climbed the steps and out of the hill into the rain and the mist for Saltersford.

At the mouth of the valley, Lankin was back in his place, as if he had never left it. Jack patted him as he went by. He crossed the Butts to Shady and down. He stopped. There was someone moving in the mist, coming towards him.

"Nan Sarah?"

She ran and clung to him.

"Jack! Whatever are you at? Your face! Jack! You're not fit! Must I have you dead twice?"

He put his free arm about her.

"Wife. Wife. Will you not be learnt?"

"But Jack! You can't be out! Not like you are! Not in this!"

"I can. And I am. And it's done. But you hear me, Nan Sarah. At times such, don't you ever go Thursbitch. You hear me? Never. It'll take a life as lief as give. It's all the same road for it up there."

16

"No, Sal. I'm not going to risk it."

"You're a wimp, Ian."

"I don't care what I am."

"You did not see a bull."

"I saw the next best."

"And I am sure that I did not see a bull. If I had, I could have remembered it."

"If you had, you wouldn't have been here to dispute it. Come on. Out. You wanted this, last time."

"Did I? What?"

"You'll see."

He parked beside the road at Pym Chair and helped her to put her hands into the loops of the trekking poles. They went through a kissing-gate to avoid the grids that spanned the road, and waited to cross. The traffic was heavy and the road narrow.

"I've never seen so many sports cars," she said.

"Male compensatory behaviour," he said.

"Then what are the bimbos expecting?" she said. "I feel sorry for them. All that randy paint on the body work and the wind in their bras."

They crossed the road and stepped up to the path for Cats Tor.

"Oh, marvellous," she said. "It's even got a dog-flap."

Immediately there was a stile.

"It's the only one," he said. "And this time we'll not try to prove anything, or there'll be a queue."

He steadied her and guided her legs and feet, and held her until she was on her poles at the other side.

"It should be all right," he said. "There's not much of a climb, and the going's firm."

"Firm? It'll be tarmac next."

"Good morning."

"Good morning."

She did not look at them.

"Good morning."

"Hello."

The courtesies came from both directions as they were overtaken.

"Ian. Don't encourage them," she said through her teeth. "It's worse than Piccadilly."

"Lovely weather."

"Isn't it! They're only being sociable."

"Sociable. Sociable I have all day. Sociable is what I've come here to get away from. Do you know what sociable is? Smile without feeling. I'm an expert on sociable, dear heart."

"Hello!"

"Hello."

"And why are they going like the clappers? Heads down as if they'd a train to catch. They ooze ethos."

"They're Doing the Tors," he said. "Shining Tor and back. It's three point two five kilometres each way."

"And that's all? Can't they see? And can't they see how abso-bloodylutely better it would be without them?"

"Think of it as a prole trap."

"Hi."

"Hello."

"Mega!"

"Know why?" she said.

"Cheers!" The walker did not pause.

"It's the Pliocene Orogeny!" she shouted.

"Cool!"

"Eventually!"

"Sal. Behave. That's enough. Do you want a smack?"

She turned to him, put her head against his chest and honked with laughter.

"I'll be good."

"Promise?"

"No."

They went on, over Cats Tor. As the next confrontation approached, she stopped, flung her hands in the air, and sang: "The hills are alive with the Sound of Mucus!"

"Good morning."

"Ian? We're not Doing the Tors, are we?"

"No. Something better. Control yourself, and you'll see. I told you."

They passed over Cats Tor, the sun in their eyes, and began the gentle descent to the ridge. The peak of Shuttlingslow was sharp in front of Mow Cop on one side and the Sutton Common radio tower on the other; but the valley stayed hidden. Andrew's Edge was dark. They followed the line of broken wall that was the county boundary.

"Slight problem," he said. "The sheep fence has been renewed. We'll have to keep going till there's a way across."

Although a try had been made at draining, in places the path was deep in water, and uneven blocks from the wall had been laid as stepping-stones. They were too unstable for her, and she had to make detours out onto the peat.

"There's a kink in the fence ahead. It looks as though there may be something."

It was a sawn-off length of telegraph pole, with the iron foot grips left in place.

"This'll do," he said. He picked her up and lifted her above the wire. She held on to the fence while he used the foot grips to climb over.

"I think you'd better bring up the rear," she said. "It's a bit too much. Sorry."

The blanket bog and boles of cotton grass were unfirm, and pockets of mud and water lay covered by reeds. He took hold of one elbow and put an arm around her shoulder.

"Wow," she said. The valley had opened. "Those few metres, and everything's different."

He took his binoculars and scanned.

"It looks safe enough," he said. "And we'd see anything in plenty of time to get clear. We need to double back on ourselves. We've overshot."

The slab of the outcrop was below them, though from the bottom of the valley it had crested the ridge.

He felt her stiffen. She paused, leaned on the poles, intent on the rock. "Yes. Yes. Yes. Yes. I remember. I do remember. Yes. Look." She placed her boot in the shallow footprint. "Look. Ian. It fits." Tears ran silent. "I've remembered. At last. Something new. Remembered."

"Can you describe the rock again?" he said.

"I could. But it's more. There's a cave."

"Is there?"

"Help me round to the front," she said. "Here. We must sit in it. We have to."

She swung off her poles into the arch and sat on the floor. He joined her in the shelter.

"You said it was natural, not hand carved. Is it?"

"Of course it is. But it's so much more."

"What do you mean?"

"Proof. Short term memory. Not gone. Not entirely. Yet. And."

"Yes?"

"It's a throne."

"I suppose it is."

"A throne of dreadful necessity."

He held her close. He watched her pick every detail from the valley.

"What about the fingernails?" he said.

"Fingernails?"

"And how long they take to grow to Andrew's Edge. Tectonic plates. Continental drift."

"Did I tell you that? I must have been showing off. I used it to try to wake up my post-grads, when all they wanted was answers. This is so much more."

"How more? What's different?"

"Me."

"Fine views, aren't they?" The man stood by the outcrop, holding a thumb-stick. They had heard no one come.

He was bearded, and wore gaitered boots, knee britches, a red anorak with PARK RANGER sewn on it and a two-way radio slotted next to his chin.

She did not look at him, but fixed her eyes unmoving on the valley.

"Yes, splendid," said Ian.

"You do know you're off the public footpath, don't you?" said the Ranger.

"Yes. But does it, in reality, matter?" he said.

"We have to be careful of the sheep in the lambing season," said the Ranger.

"Which is why, surely, there are no sheep up here now. They've been taken down to the bottom, where the public access is clearly marked."

The Ranger laughed.

"OK. It's as much routine to keep the litter under control. Help yourselves, please. And enjoy the day. But, in future, I'd be happier if you cleared things with the farmers first."

He turned to go.

"Of course we shall. That was unthinking. But talking about people being stupid: I should tell you that there was a bull loose in the valley when we were here last."

"A bull? There can't have been," said the Ranger. "It's illegal in a public place."

"That's my point."

"Where did you see it?"

"We didn't see it. But the droppings were north of the ford, on this side."

"I'm afraid you must have been mistaken. No bull has been reported."

"I'm reporting it. And I assure you, I am one that knows his turds."

The Ranger grinned, then frowned. "When was this?"

"Two weeks ago today."

"The only bull is at Longclough," said the Ranger. "It's kept up, and I check regularly. Do you want me to file an incident report?"

"I think it might be as well."

"I'll double check that fencing now, in any case."

The Ranger lifted his stick in greeting and left them.

"Thanks, Ian."

"He was doing his job. And I'm used to being an escaped goat."

"I was with the valley. Of the valley. And the valley was with me: of me."

"I know. And where is the place of understanding?"

"All right. But don't start getting professional now. Please."

17

With the first nine stars, the people led their cattle towards Jenkin from the farms around. Across the lane, wood and bones were stacked together, and cut turves piled apart. The cattle were penned with hurdles as they arrived, and the people gathered in silence before Jenkin.

Martha Barber gave a bundle of cloth to Jack. He unrolled the bundle and held the two sticks that were in it. One was flat, with a charred hollow at its centre; the other was rounded and the charring was at one pointed end.

Jack laid the flat stick on the ground and knelt on one knee, holding the stick firm with the other foot. He took the rounded stick, placed the sharp end in the hollow, and began to roll it between his palms, backwards and forwards, fast, not stopping. The people watched. The only sounds were the restless shifting of the cattle and the whirling of the wood. Though small, it made a noise that echoed from Jenkin's face: a rhythm of the air itself breathing, roaring.

Jack did not falter, but watched. He nodded, and Martha Barber crumbled dried heather into the hole. Soon a smoke rose, and she trickled more of the heather dust. The smoke became white, and at the last pale of the day a glow appeared in the wood. Martha lifted grass in her hand and held it close. A brief flame ran; but before it died she bent over with heather sprigs and caught the flame. Mary Turner brought more; and between them they passed the flame from thicker to thicker sprigs, until Martha Barber held a torch. She gave the torch to Jack, and he lit the heather inside the stack of wood and bone, so that the fire took and the stack became a blaze.

The fire shone from the whiteness of Jenkin, and the curled stones in the rock gleamed.

Then the people sang, and the young men and bigger boys jumped through the flames, and, laughing, chased the girls and dragged them to leap hand in hand with them back over the bones.

When they had caught all that they could, they opened up the fire and drove the cattle through. The light was in the bellowing and the eyes, and the panicked beasts scattered to the pastures.

The people gathered the embers, and each family lifted a turf from the stack and carried the turf to the fire. Then, still singing, they walked back to their hearths, spreading out from Jenkin under the stars, holding stars in their hands, kindling summer.

Martha Barber wrapped the two sticks into their bundle and went her way.

18

"I am not happy about this."

"I am," she said.

"It is impractical."

"Ian, it's the opposite. And it's pragmatic. No one can say how much more my legs have got, and still less about me. It's warm and fine, but the days are shorter. Next month it won't be possible. I've not seen the valley at night, and this could be my last chance. Get that bull out of your bonnet, and at least let's give it a try. I promise not to argue."

"Is it so important?"

"It is so important."

"Why?"

"It's the only thing I can remember. Time is breaking," she said. "I can't read any more. Three pages and I've forgotten what the book's about. It's the same with the telly. I can watch a film over and over, and don't know what's going to happen next. I can't keep enough in my head to follow a reasoned paper, not even when it's written by someone I once taught. Music still works. And here. At first it was as bad as anywhere. But I've remembered even what I'd forgotten. Don't you see what that means to me? Outside, all I have is what I knew before this started. Now, nothing stays. I feel safe with the valley. And I want to know its stars."

Thursbitch was in shadow by the time they reached the entrance. Only the high tops and the ridge held the sun. Andrew's Edge was black. The first sheets of mist were lying among the reeds. The sky was blue metalled above and in front, and behind them red without cloud. The smells of the valley were stronger, and bees worked the flowers to the last of the light.

They went slowly, not talking. The poles bore most of her weight and he held her arm and the belt around her waist to steady her. It was as though her body were struggling to walk and to dance at the same time, so that her feet placed themselves, whether right or wrong, and her head turned from side to side, making her move her eyes to keep a straight way.

He climbed over the stile. She lay upright against it and he lifted her and brought her across.

"I must go to the well," she said, "before the light fades."

"Will you be able to manage on the wet?"

"Yes. I remember the well. And the big stones where we got lost. And the outcrop on the ridge. Didn't I forget it once?"

They laughed.

"See. It's not all bad. I remember forgetting. But I can't remember whether I was always forgetful."

"I don't think we should try for the row of stones," he said. "The ground is too rough."

"The well is what matters."

They passed over the ford and went around the reed beds as far as they could to reach the well. They stood above the fallen masonry. The water running under the roof slab was louder than the brook next to it.

She looked up at the opposite ridge. The line was dark against the darkening blue, and the outcrop sharp.

"When we first came, you saw a connection," he said.

"Between what?"

"Here and there."

"Did I?"

"A connection of difference, you said. Two same shapes, two features, but one natural and the other made. You were right. The outcrop's high and hollow and moves outwards. The well's here and hollow and moves in."

"You're learning, Ian. That's what I came to see. I know it now. Let's go and sit."

She turned herself away on her poles.

They went back to the ford and sat against the stone at its headland above the water.

"Coffee?"

"Please."

He opened the Thermos flask and kept hold of the lid while she put her hands round his and drank. They ate some of the sandwiches.

"What time is it?" she said.

"Half past eight."

"I'd better get pilled up. If I go to sleep, wake me."

She unzipped a pocket in her anorak and took out a dispensing box. She shook several differently coloured tablets from a compartment and swallowed them with the coffee.

"I can see a star!" It was high above the outcrop. As the night closed on the valley, more stars appeared and the one star became a constellation.

"It's Deneb in Cygnus," he said.

She watched the sky, childlike, pointing at first, but soon quiet, and looking, and listening, while the sky filled.

"Why is it I don't forget this place?"

"I've no idea."

"It's stronger even than I thought. Once I'd remembered, it felt as though things were coming back to me that I had not learned."

"I'm afraid, Sal, that sounds more like your subjectivity interacting with your symptoms."

"Probably."

The sky moved round.

"Ian? How good are you on Quantum Theory?"

"No good at all. It's an area I feel I should be more aware of. As with most things."

"I must have touched on it once; otherwise I shouldn't be able to ask you now."

"So?"

"It's gone. But I've got this niggle that it could be connected to why this place knows we're here."

"You are not still serious about that, are you?"

"Of course I am. Most geologists agree about sentient landscape. If you do enough fieldwork, you can't avoid it. Some places have to be treated with respect, though that doesn't get written up in the literature."

"Come off it."

"Are you telling me, after all we've seen and done here, that this is just any old gritstone anticline?"

"I'd say that it's a powerful and dramatic sub-Alpine environment. But what I accept as appearing to be a strong atmosphere is no more than our projection of our own experience and emotion onto a circum- scribed place."

"How can a man with your job talk such crap?"

"You have to bear in mind I'm also a scientist."

"Bollocks. This place scares the shite out of you."

"Have another sandwich, and watch the stars."

They leaned their heads against the stone. The sky turned.

"What's happening at the outcrop?" she said.

"Nothing? The Pleiades are rising to the northeast. Taurus will be up soon."

"I'm not imagining. That rock's got a halo."

"It has to be coincidence."

A waning moon rose from the outcrop, from the cave within.

"That is spectacular. If we were anywhere else but here, at this stone, we should not be seeing this effect. It has to be coincidence, because the only alternative would be that the stone was put here in order to provoke the phenomenon."

"I think it's just a big dick," she said.

"Mm."

"Now it's your turn."

"To what?"

"To mm."

They sat and watched, not speaking. A fox came down to drink at the ford, caught their scent and looked at them, and walked, unhurried, away. A hare went up the field across the brook. Taurus lifted from the ridge and its red eye hung above the outcrop.

"Dark and true and tender is the North," she said. "I must have learnt that. Once."

"Mm."

"Mm?"

"A hunch, that's all," he said. "Do you think we could go a short way up there?"

"Fine."

He helped her to stand. They took a torch, but left the bag by the stone.

"Say if it gets too much."

They wove across the field, up to the wall that marked the rough pasture, to the bellied stone.

"Is this why?" she said. "If so, I'm sitting down."

"Mm."

"Ian, what are you humming about?"

"Just a thought. I'm out of my depth. But, if you take the site of the outcrop as fixed then, by observation and the placing of markers, it would be possible to make accurate calculations of time."

"For what purpose?"

"I don't know. Whatever. For a reason good enough to lug these stones around."

"And who would do that?"

"But they probably don't work now as they were meant to, if they ever were meant to."

"Why?"

"The earth shifts on its axis."

"I thought it was just me."

"That moon really was impressive. And from here, Bellatrix is clearing the outcrop. Which means that Orion will rise, though we'll scarcely see it. Dawn's not – Look out!"

He pushed her round and held her against the stone with his body. There was a thumping above in the heather, and rocks crashed into the wall, some bouncing over into the field.

"Fools! Stop it! Stop! You'll kill someone!"

More rocks came tumbling; and then there was a loud, drawn out cry.

"Sheep," he said. "They dislodged the scree."

"There isn't any scree," she said. "And that wasn't sheep."

The cry came again, desolate. Then silence.

"A fox."

Something landed in the heather and rolled to the back of the stone. He shone his torch. It was a small lump of rock, but different. He picked it up and gave it to her, lighting it with the torch.

"This isn't from anywhere near here," she said. "It's carbon fluoride. And it's been hollowed. Stick your torch inside."

The stone glowed white and violet. It was rough on the outside, but had been polished within.

"It's a cup. Of sorts," he said.

"You find this colour only in the carboniferous limestone at Tray Cliff, outside Castleton. The miners call it bull-beef. So there is someone up there. Or there was."

They waited, but there was neither sound nor movement. Over Cats Tor there was a brightening in the sky. They began the slow way down to the brook.

At the stone above the ford they drank more coffee and finished the food. Orion was waist-high from the outcrop, but faded from their sight before he was free.

"Let's watch the sun rise," she said. "Then I shall have known it all."

He arranged the bag so that the stone cup was protected. Behind them, the light crept down Andrew's Edge. She sat forward, holding herself with expectation.

The sun rose.

The sun rose clear from the outcrop, as the moon before it.

"It's functional," he said.

"It's wonderful."

"I simply don't have the maths."

"Who needs it? Just look. What day is it?"

"Thursday."

"I mean, is it significant?"

"I haven't the slightest idea. But. No, that's irrelevant."

"What is?"

He looked in his diary.

"The only thing I can think of is that today happens to be the Feast of the Decollation of Saint John the Baptist. Which doesn't exactly sit comfortably with the notion of problematic stones."

"I need to move," she said. "The valley and the pills are telling me."

He lifted her and they left the ford. The air was all new, and the light fresh, bringing back the colours of the place.

She looked up at the ridge.

"That noise."

"Wasn't it?" he said. "But foxes can make frightening sounds."

"Not a fox. It was a man. I heard him. I heard what he said. He was calling: 'Wife'."

19

"Early Monday morning, late on Saturday night,
  I saw ten thousand mile away a house just out of sight!
  The floor was on the ceiling, the front was at the back;
  It stood alone between two more,
  And the walls were whitewashed black!"
He raised his hat to Jenkin as they passed the stone.

  "I am a roving jagger,
  And fightable to rights;
  I travel countries far and near,
  And march by days and nights.
  I travel countries far and near,
  As you may understand,
  Until at last I do arrive
  On The Red Erythræan Strand!"
He was close enough to set the dogs barking.

  "O I'm a blade
  As knows no trade,
  And folks they do adore me!
  I'll shoe their feet, I won't them cheat,
  But they'll not reach home before me!
  For I can sing and I can dance,
  I am that roving jagger;
  If Trouble ever should me chance,
  I'll stick him with me dagger!"

Nan Sarah came down the path into the lane. She put her arms about him.

"I thought I'd not see you again."

"There, there, love. Have I not told you often enough? I'm the one as always comes back. I gave word to a chap, telling you I'd be away. Did he not?"

"He did. But he didn't tell where you were for."

"I met a man at Derby, and he was lost to take a jag down south; so I must give him a hand. And one road leads to another, they say. My, woman, but you're biggening."

"You've been gone that long."

"Let me see to me beasts now; and then I'll tell you all about me little periploos. I could sup a jug of ale."

He unloaded the horses, watered and fed them, gave Bryn a bone, and went into the houseplace. Richard Turner and Mary were sitting on either side of the fire.

"Now then, youth."

"Now then, Father."

"Yon was a tragwallet and a bit."

"Above a bit. But it made a mighty penny."

"That's what counts."

"So you did get a second bite off his head, I see."

"We did. An abundation. Yon good slobber of rain fixed us nicely. And yours is in, too. High Medda and all."

"Grand. And I picked the corbel bread, gen next year, on me way up from Chester." He set apart a bag of red and white toadstools.

"What have you fetched us?" said Mary.

"Now why should a man as has been down London be at fetching trinklements all that road? It's jag enough, without trinklements on top."

"London?" said Mary. "What's that?"

"Where King is."

"Who's he now?" said Richard Turner.

"And a right midden of a place, I can tell you," said Jack. "I don't know how he tholes it, King. I was glad to be shut; I was that."

"What did you see, Jack?" said Nan Sarah.

He looked around, and then leaned forward, pulling them in to hear.

"I saw houses thatched with pancakes, walls of pudding pies; and little pigs running in the streets with knives and forks in their backs, saying, 'Who'll have a slice?'."

"Did you?" said Nan Sarah.

Richard Turner laughed, spat in the fire and settled back in his chair.

"He's twitting you," said Mary.

"Jack?"

Jack drank deeply from the jug, his eyes bright above the rim.

"Jack! You great nowt!"

She pummelled his chest.

"Do you not want to hear of me little periploos?" he said. "Me periploos of The Red Erythræan Sea?"

He lifted his satchel onto the table.

"There's nowt as can beat a good periploos for telling strange tales and finding rum things and hearing daft songs. And this one's had them all. There's some folks with thoughts fit to grow wooden legs; I'll tell you. Now where's the old powsels and thrums?" He rummaged about. "Powsels and thrums. Powsels and thrums. Right. Now then, Father, what do you make of this?"

He put into Richard Turner's hand an oval brass box. The lid was sunken, without any way of opening it. Richard Turner tried to slip his fingernail in, but it was too coarse. He shook it; there was no sound.

"Fetch us a knife."

"No, Father. What should you do if you were up the fields with this here, and no knife? You'd still want it open."

Richard Turner held the box every way, looking for a button or a catch, but the box was smooth, with only the outline of the sunken lid. He laughed.

"Nay, youth. Yon's reckoned me up."

"Hold it in your hand, Father, and thrutch both sides at same time. Not too hard, mind; but hard enough."

Richard Turner set the box in his palm and squeezed. Nothing happened.

"Too much," said Jack.

He squeezed again.

"Too little."

Both men were laughing.

"Trust you, our Jack, to make a man's life a misery. Eh!" The lid sprang wide on a hinge, and Richard Turner nearly dropped the box. "Well, I'll go to the foot of our stairs!"

"Poke your nutting-hook in that, Father."

"There's near an eight ounce o' bacca, youth!"

"There'd best be," said Jack, "else there'll be a chap wanting his face mending next time I see him."

"It's a grand un. Spon spitting-fire new." Richard Turner closed and opened the box, over and over, chuckling. "As good a job as any I've seen in many a long day."

"Ay, well," said Jack. "So one of you's suited, and that's a mercy. Now what? Powsels and thrums. Powsels and thrums. Here we are. Will this do you, Ma Mary?"

He brought out a looking glass in a wooden frame and handle and gave it to her with the back upwards. Mary took it, turned it over and squealed.

"Our Jack! I've heard tell on 'em! Eh, Rutchart."

She held it up to him.

"Who's that smart chap?" said Richard Turner. "By, he's a fine figure of a man, isn't he? It'd be a lucky woman as could catch him. Wouldn't it, Nan Sarah?"

He showed her the glass. "Barm pot," she said, but peered closely into it before giving it back to Mary. "What's for me, Jack?" Her face was flushed.

"What's for you?" Jack looked at her belly. "Haven't I given you enough already?"

"Jack!"

"I don't know. I do not know. You're a bucket with no bottom, you." He lifted the satchel. "Light as a feather. Feels empty. Let's see. Powsels and thrums. No. Nowt. Wait on. There's an old muckender, if that's any good to you."

He pulled out a dirty handkerchief. It was crumpled and knotted. He looked into the satchel, and shook it over the table.

"No. You'll have to make do, Nan Sarah."

His face was mournful.

Nan Sarah took the handkerchief. She tried to unfasten the knot, but it was firmly tied. She struggled and tugged.

"Oh, Jack!"

"I tell you. It's this or nowt. A man has more to think on than trinklements when he's leading a full jag."

She pushed at the knot, and it began to loosen. She worked on the rag with her teeth, and it moved. The handkerchief opened of itself from within and was covered by a blossoming unfolding of red, embroidered with flowers and bees, yellow and black and white and green.

"What is it?"

"You tell me, Nan Sarah."

"Is it silk?"

"It is that."

"But silk's white."

"It is while other folks get their hands on it. You're a throwster. What happens next?"

"You take it for spinners down Macc, and fetch another brood of grubs."

"Then what?"

"They give it weavers."

"Then what?"

"It gets woven."

"Then what?"

"How should I know? I've seen old buttons."

"Oh, Nan Sarah, do you never think? Throwster gives spinner. Spinner gives weaver. What's it all for?"

"Summat or other."

"Woman, woman. That's how folks make their fortunes. It's dyed, and cut, and sewn; and kings and queens and suchlike wear it."

"Do they?"

"They do. And yon's for why I've fetched you this. So as a throwster can be as grand as any."

"But what is it?"

"Pockets."

"It's never pockets. Pockets are in your britches."

"But, down London, it's what them fine ladies wear, I'm told."

Nan Sarah opened up the silk.

It was a belt, and from it hung two deep pouches, all in red. In each was a slit running down from the top to the middle, and every seam and edge was stitched in green. Patterns of yellow flowers on green stems were interlaced, with petals marked and hued, and among the flowers hung bees, the wings embroidered white, with every vein clear.

"Jack. It's gorgeous. How must I wear it?"

"I'm told sideways."

"I've got no sideways!"

"Down London, ladies put them under their skirts and petticoats."

"What?" said Nan Sarah. "You mean none of this shows?"

"Well, I never saw any," said Jack. "I got all this off a Frenchie as didn't talk too much English. It makes you wonder how them lot manage. He seemed in a bit of a hurry, so it didn't take much to knock him down. He was glad enough with me malt. And I always like to leave a chap happy and smiling."

"I'll not wear them under," said Nan Sarah. "Let's give Lomases summat to talk about. Lend us a hand, Jack."

Jack put the belt around Nan Sarah and tied it in a bow. The pockets sat on her hips.

"It's a good job I came when I did," he said. "Another three-week and you'd have had to wait."

Nan Sarah lifted her arms to show off the pockets.

"You look well," said Mary. "But if they're pockets for ladies, what shall you put in them?"

"Me hands," said Nan Sarah.

She thrust them deep into the pockets, and skipped around, holding them out.

Mary sat with the looking glass and made different faces in it. Richard Turner filled his pipe, staring into the fire.

Jack went to settle the horses. Nan Sarah followed, her hands still in the pockets.

"Yon young youth," said Richard Turner. "He's got a boggart in him. Don't ask me: but in him there is a boggart."

"Time for bed, wife."

"Yes, Jack."

"So they'll do, will they?"

"They'll do, love."

Still with her hands inside the silk, she took hold of him, and they danced together into their room, and kissed. He undid the bow and she folded the pockets and put them on a chair. He snuffed out the rush light.

"Has there been any foreigners while I was gone, Nan Sarah?"

"Above a few jaggers, but none as we don't know."

"I saw a couple of chaps standing up Thoon when I was coming down Todd Hill," he said. "I couldn't make nowt of 'em, except one was on two sticks. How does a chap on two sticks get up Thoon? But from me to them the distance was savage."

"No. There's been none like that."

"Savage. Oh, wife, each night of all them miles, how I have missed you. But if I never went, how could I come home?"

20

They were doing the autumn jobs.

"There's some thackstones loose," Jack said. "I'll fetch the ladder."
He climbed onto the roof and walked around, checking the slabs.
Some he slid into place on their latts; others had lost their bone pegs
and he took fresh ones and set them in their holes. Richard Turner
watched from below.

"We need two narrow ladies, Father, for close by the chimney; one
rogue-why-wink-thee, a small duchess, a wide countess, a short
haghatty; and we'd best have a twothree bachelors. I'll give you a
hand."

Richard Turner went to the stone stack to sort out the different
sizes. The smaller pieces he carried to the ladder, while Jack walked
the heavier slabs on their corners. They put the stones in a sling on
the end of a rope, and Jack went back to the roof, while Richard
Turner climbed the ladder and guided the sling. It took six loads to
get the pieces up.

Once on the roof, they moved together, gentle and slow, not to slip,
and so that no fixed stones were damaged. They had to prise firm
slabs to take out each broken one and peg in the new. It was all heavy
work on the pitch of the roof.

"Father?"

"Ay?"

"What's Sin?"

"How do you mean, sin?"

"It's summat to do with churches, I reckon; and you've been Taxal and Macc. What are they for?"

"They're bury-holes."

"Then what are steeples?"

"So as you can tell where the bury-hole is, and folks don't go traipsing round all day carrying dead uns."

"But I see ever so many when I'm leading me jags."

"That'll be on account of having ever so many dead uns. They'd not all fit in Taxal and Macc. I recollect you can get wed there, too, if you've a mind and can find a parson. There had used to be a lot on it one time o' day, I do believe. Quite a curfuffle. Me father had used to talk of it. And his father had used to say there was a big to-do once. But it was always summat and nowt, in my youth. And there's none of it goes on as makes any odds now. Why do you ask?"

"Down Derby and places, I've seen churches thrunk with folk, and bells ringing. What are they at?"

"Oh, I'll grant you, there's many as like to get together and sing their little ditties. But in these parts, it'd be a day's work to fetch enough on us for make a cat laugh."

"But what's Sin?"

"Don't be daft, youth. Yon's a word; same as, It's long sin we had such a storm. Or, It's a while sin you gave me this here thackstone to hold while you rambled and romped with your mither."

Jack chuckled, pegged the stone and fitted it over the latt.

When they had done, they climbed down and sat in the lee of the wind and smoked their pipes. The day was golden.

Richard Turner dozed. Jack looked out over Park Meadow up to Buxter Stoops, but his eyes were seeing beyond. He took a short stick out of his britches. At the top was a drum, deeply carved, and above that a knob, or an acorn, or a bud. From the edge of the drum hung a wooden bead on a chain. Jack worked the handle with his wrist, and the drum began to spin. As it spun faster, the bead moved outwards on its chain, and the weight of it made the spinning easier. The drum whirred. Jack saw further through the tobacco smoke.

Richard Turner half opened one eye.

"And what's yon huzzing effort?"

"It's me little whizzler," said Jack.

"And what's it for?"

"I don't know. Nor did the chap I got it off. He didn't think much on it, so I did him a favour. It helps me think. And me beasts follow it. And there's times when a man's weary and feeling far from home; and then it can put him right for another day. There's all manner of thing can be fetched round a fire at night, if a man looks."

He watched the spinning drum.

"I saw some queer chaps this last jag, Father."

"Oh, ay?"

"They kept jumping up at markets and flustering folks. But folks were moths in a candle wi' 'em, and having a right good skrike and acting feart."

"Oh, ay?"

"Where's sense in being feart and skriking, and then shouting as they'd had a right good time? I heard 'em."

"And what were these chaps on about?"

"They were promising as we were all going to burn in big ovens when we die, because we were all born nowty, and there was some governor as had it in for us, choose how much we said we were sorry. But sorry for what? No matter o' that, his gang were going to shovel us in ovens and roast us on forks, day and night for evermore. Leastways, that's what I made on it. But these chaps were chelping all the same tatherum-y-dyal, I couldn't rightly say what they were at. First one as I heard, I thought he was just bad luck top end. But if he was, there's many same as him now. And folks seemed to be enjoying theirselves. Why? That's what I can't plunder. Where are they from? And is it catching?"

"I can't find any from where I'm sitting," said Richard Turner. "So I'll not lose sleep on it. Twiddle yon huzzer at 'em, next time, and tell 'em to get away with their bother. Bezonter me! Here's a sight for sore eyes!"

Nan Sarah was waddling down the lane from Jenkin. She had her pockets round her, hands still in them, and the red silk gleamed as she waved.

"And where've you been?" said Richard Turner. "Is there no work to be done?"

"It's such a grand day," said Nan Sarah. "I thought I'd go over to Lomases and see if they were well."

Jack stood and put away the drum.

"Nan Sarah. Woman. I don't know why I bother."

They laughed, and she took one hand out of its pocket to put round his neck. He held her wrist.

"What's them?"

There was a ring of red spots under the frill of her sleeve.

"Flefs," she said. "Now give us a kiss."

21

She sat in the car and made no move, but looked out at the hills and into her bag.

"What have you got there?" he said.

"My new hat. Do you like it? It's *de rigueur*. I have to wear it all the time when I'm out now. Help me put it on."

She handed him the padded helmet. He fitted it around her head, and fastened the chin piece.

She adjusted the mirror.

"I'd look fine on a bike," she said. "It's better quality than they're wearing."

A string of cyclists from Saltersford crested Pym Chair, crouched over their narrow handlebars.

"Watch it, lads!" she shouted. "It plays all hell-up with your sperm count!"

She was inert again.

"Where do you want to go?" he said.

Her head moved and rolled, almost a grin.

"Do you want to go along the ridge?"

"No."

"Do you want to go to the valley?"

"Yes."

He drove back down towards Jenkin Chapel and left the road at Howlersknowl. He helped her out and onto the poles.

"You must be sick and bloody tired of this," she said.

"Not in the least."

"You are. I know you are. I can tell."

"I am not going to argue, Sal."

"But I am! It's just bloody brownie points! So you can go back feeling moral! God, you're so bloody virtuous! How dare you feel sorry for me? You make me sick! You and your bloody vocation! Bloody sanctimonious bastards!"

"I do not feel sorry for you."

"Show some emotion, damn you! You, you do it all in your head! The rest of us have to do it out in a real world! Christ Alcrappingmighty! And those notes! What are you going to make of them? Write a best-seller? Become an authority? Have your own website? And why not? Help yourself! Mate! You've put enough hours in! I hate you! I hate your self-righteous bloody face! You calm, smug, wanking shit! Shit! Shit! You ineffable shit!"

"I'd rather it were more uneffingly, Sal."

"Oh, Ian." She turned to him. "Don't hide with words. You scare me when you twist them. I think it's me not getting it right. Silly Sally. Sally Malley. Silly Sally Malley."

She sobbed and laughed. He held her and lowered her onto a boulder by the track.

"We sat here, before," she said. "There's a ring in the stone. It pinched."

"There isn't one now," he said. "But you're right. It was this stone. And I saw a ring, too." They looked at the yellow top. It was smooth, with spreads of lichen. "There's no sign of there ever having been anything. It's weathered evenly."

"Well, there we are, then," she said. "At least we're dementing together. Let's walk. I want you to make a promise."

"What promise?"

"Let's walk."

They climbed into the valley. She stopped and leaned on the poles and against him.

"Ian. Thanks. You're kind."

"Sal, I am not kind. That is not what I am. Thanks are not appropriate. You are what matters."

She looked at him sideways, and they walked on.

"I want to go to that stone again," she said.

"Which?"

"Where we heard the man calling."

"Where we heard something."

"Where I heard the man calling."

"There's plenty of time," he said.

"Is there, indeed?"

They tracked across the slope from the ruin up to the stone. He helped her to sit with her back straight.

"What a golden day," she said.

"Do you want to eat?"

"No. We must make the most of it before the cold."

She watched patterns of cloud and sun on the slope across the brook and the swing of the shadow of Andrew's Edge. She waved her hand.

"There's someone by that old well. Looking at us."

"I can't see anybody."

"They've moved."

"They?"

"He. She. It."

"What did you mean by a promise, Sal?"

"What promise?"

"Nothing. Do you want to eat?"

"Yes."

"Drink first. I've brought your cup."

He took the stone out of his bag.

"Let me have a proper look. Turn it over. Aha. It is carbon fluoride. Organic staining gives it that colour. And it is Tray Cliff bull-beef."

"But what is it? What is it for?"

"There's quite a tourist industry. I wonder why he threw it away. It'll have cost him."

"Who?"

"The man I heard."

"It's honey and water mixed," he said. "Yes?"

"Fine."

He poured the thick liquid from the Thermos into the stone cup and gave her a drinking straw. He held the cup as she drank.

"I'll save some," she said.

He unwrapped the sandwiches. Half of them were cut into small squares. She opened her mouth.

"Breathe in first, Sal."

He put a square to the side of her tongue.

"Close your mouth."

"It's – "

"Don't talk until you've swallowed. Right. Have another drink."

"It's hard to chew," she said.

"That's why you must take your time."

"Time, time, time. It seems to be in every sentence. Then I suppose it is."

"Drink?"

"Yes. But my feet need anchoring. Any of those stones will do."

He put a flat wall stone across each instep.

"Sit straight again, Sal; and tuck your chin in. Now. Open."

22

"Land man was here while you were gone," said Richard Turner.

"Was he?" said Jack. "And what did that high-learnt letter gent have to say for himself?"

"He was a new un; one of the best of the worser kind of folk. T'other chap died seven year back, seemingly."

"I wondered we'd been spared."

"Yay, but now we've a young master all set to be a green broom."

"He'll want some learning, then."

Jack and his father were bringing the cattle down from the summer pasture. The dogs were with them.

"He will," said Richard Turner. "He's a sprightly youth, full of newfanglements. Not a patch on that old un, as took as he was told."

"What did he think on us?"

"He had to find summat wrong, o' cause. Shippon doors must be mended; and Bean Croft wants liming. This and t'other. But he was decent enough, in his way, from what I could make on him. They talk that far back, some on 'em, a man can't hardly plunder where they're at. He gave Tally Ridge a bit of what-for; but he said he'd write our place a good word for Lord Cag-mag, bless him."

"And rent?"

"Oh, he's putting that up, and no error. He wants more; he does that. For improvements, he said."

"Is old chap going to build himself a castle, then?"

"No. It's for here. He said."

"What wants improvements here?"

Richard Turner did not answer.

"Father?"

"I said he was sprightly. Not like others, as you could send along the brook from Nab End to Toddscliff and back and leave 'em be. This one was at looking for himself."

"Where?"

"All over."

"You're holding summat, Father. What is it?"

"He's for taking in every inch of land; walling right up Tors."

"He can't do that."

"He says he can."

"What's the use? He can't wall them places. Them hills. They'll not wear it."

Richard Turner was silent.

"Father? You never showed him Thursbitch?"

"There was no need, youth. He found it. And how could we stop him? He's for taking it in, cutting it up, setting drains. He says he'll make it a farm and build a house there."

"He can't do that, Father."

"I'm of opinion for to think as how nowt can stop that one. He's set on it. What tickled his fancy were us high stones. He's for raunging 'em out, mostly. And what's left, he says, will do champion for setting field lines and gates and that."

"He can't, Father. Never. He can't. If he does, it'll be a land of great absence."

"We tried to tell him. But he wouldn't be. We all did. But there's things as we can't tell, isn't there?"

"And where's this house he's going to build?"

"At the ford. Agen old Thrumble."

"Damn it and sink it, Father! No!"

"But what's to be done, Jack?"

"He can go for a short walk on a long night. That's what."

"It'd not help. He took drawings back with him."

Jack squatted on his heel.

"Damn it and sink it. I should've been here. I should've been here. I never should have went."

"You couldn't have done nowt, youth," said Richard Turner.

"Could I not? Could I not just! Father, you take your kyne down."

Jack climbed back to the Tors, and up. He stood at the ford.

> "A water is as I must pass.
>
> A broader water never was.
>
> Yet of all waters I did see,
>
> To pass over with less jeopardy."

He crossed to Bully Thrumble, and went from Bully Thrumble to Pearly Meg's and down the steps. He raised his hat for the darkness, and took the wooden tube from his satchel and chewed and swallowed three stems; and dipped his hat in the well and drank four crownsful. Then he went back to the stone, and sat, and waited.

He spoke to Thoon.

"O white Bull. O worthy Bull. O noble Bull. O bonny Bull, as lives on hill tops. O striding Bull, as lives on hill tops. O Bull, as in whose highmost step drops honey. Lord over all as close the eye. Say now what must be done, sin you can do owt. Yet don't you sneap them as can't know. It's on me, not them. Anyroad, that's it."

He waited. The stone of Bully Thrumble grew cold and dry to his hand, but alive. He stood against it. There was a rustling in the grass and in the reeds. Each one sound was small, but there were so many that he heard them as a great wind with no breath. He looked, and all the earth heaved with snakes coming from Pearly Meg's. They came to him, and he did not shift, but turned his eyes towards Thoon.

The snakes coiled over his shoes and climbed his legs. They wove about above and below and up to his neck and along his arms and around the stone, binding the two. They worked inside his clothes, and their dryness was smooth on his skin. They held his neck but did not squeeze, and were plaited in his hair. A head entered his mouth and throat, but it did not choke him, into his lungs, through his veins, down to his belly. Each nostril was filled, but still he breathed. They were his ears, and whispered to him their last secret. "The Bull is father to the Snake: the Snake is to the Bull." The deathless life became his life, so that he knew nothing of him but all that was within and without was one, and the rock and well were one, and the sky and the waters were one, and death and life were one, and he was of them all; and there was no ending of them.

He saw. And, with his understanding, the snakes drew back and left him. Yet something still held. He looked down. The stone, his body, his face were in a net of ivy.

He pulled himself from it. The suckers were on the stone, on his clothes and under them. He ripped from his face and hair and beard, taking no note of the pain. He stripped and tore and spat the ivy.

Then he went down from Thursbitch.

He found Richard Turner in the brewis.

"Father, I've set all to rights."

"Have you now? And how did you manage that?"

"I've promised."

"You've promised what?"

"I've promised to do what's needed."

"And who've you promised?" He went up to Jack and looked into his face. "Oh ay. That sort of a promise. I see. Well, you think on. Don't you be setting yourself up above what you can't thole, and then. Promise is nowt afore doing. And doing can come by a road you're not looking for. You're nobbut a man, when all's said. And what's up yonder drives a pretty bargain. And who are you to say what's needed? It could call for a pocket deeper nor what you've got."

"Pockets?" Nan Sarah came from the houseplace. "You've not fetched more, have you?" She was still wearing hers. "Jack! Wherever have you been? You look as if you were pulled through a hedge backwards. Come here with you."

She brushed the green leaves from him. Richard Turner went into the houseplace.

"Give over, woman," said Jack, and lifted her hands away. "Now what's all this?"

Her wrists were ringed with small, flat, dry, black blisters.

"It's nowt," she said.

He touched one, and it flaked off.

"I told you. It's nowt."

23

"Ma Mary, will you come and look?"

Mary went into Jack and Nan Sarah's room, wearing her night-gown. Nan Sarah was in bed, and there was the one rush lit.

"What is it?"

"I don't know. But summat's up. She went to bed with a sick headache, and now one minute she says she's cold, and next she's too hot, and now she's sleeping."

"She's been that road for a day or two," said Mary. "Sitting by the fire and counting pothooks. I doubt it's no more than her condition and a touch o' fever. I've not seen her eat much."

"But she drinks like I don't know what."

"There you are, then. Same as they say. Feed a cold and starve a fever. Let her sleep and she'll be right as rain by morning."

"But what are these here?" said Jack. He pulled Nan Sarah's hair to one side and held the light close. "She's got plums on her neck." At the side of the neck there were small red and black swellings.

"I'll fetch Father."

She left the room. Nan Sarah half woke.

"Jack. I'm going to be sick again."

He held the bowl for her, and she vomited.

Mary came back with Richard Turner. They both had candlesticks. Nan Sarah put a hand over her eyes.

"Light's hurting."

Mary moved the hair back, and Richard Turner looked closely. "Nay!"

He caught Mary by the arm and hurried her from the room and down the stairs.

"Father!"

"It's Great Mortality!"

Jack went to the top of the stair.

"Father!"

"Great Mortality! Them's plums as ride on flesh wi' savage jaws!"

Richard Turner and Mary were in the houseplace, with the door shut. Jack was alone on the stair in darkness.

"What are you meaning?"

"Great Mortality! Out! Out!"

"Father?"

"Out! Both on you!"

"Father! Have you lost your wits?"

"Out!"

"Jack? What's up?"

"Hush, love."

"Jack. I'm badly."

"Out!"

Jack went to Nan Sarah. She was sitting on the bed. "It's me father. I don't know what's taken him."

"Nay, Rutchart, nay!"

"Leave me!"

The door of the houseplace was opened and a dim light was on the stair.

"Jack!" Richard Turner called from below. "Yon's Great Mortality! Get her from here! Out! Now! Be told!"

"She's badly!"

"Be told!"

Jack went to the stair again. There was a flash and an explosion and the smell of powder.

"Rutchart!"

"Be told, youth!"

"I'm on the stairs."

"Come no nearer!"

"He's got both guns!" shouted Mary.

"Out! Now!"

Jack went back to Nan Sarah.

"Me father's mad. I fear he'll shoot us. There's no reasoning with him. Dress, wife. Take some things, and we'll try again in daylight when he's mebbe come to his senses."

He went to the stair again.

"Father?"

"Out!"

"We're going now. I'm taking the dog, and two of me beasts, and some bread and cheese."

"Nay!"

Shadows changed in the dimness, and Jack heard Richard Turner go to the brewis door and open it. Then he went back to the house-place.

"You touch dog or beast, and I must shoot 'em!"

The door of the houseplace closed. Mary was talking to Richard Turner. His voice did not soften. His words were muffled, but Jack heard the fear.

He took Nan Sarah down the stair and through the brewis. The houseplace door opened, and he stopped. The silhouette of Richard Turner showed a levelled gun.

"You'll not do this, Father."

"Yay but I must, youth. For all on us. We'll know soon enough who's safe."

"What is it?"

"There's not time. Get you gone."

Jack heard the cocking of the flint.

"Don't you hurt Ma Mary."

"I shall not that."

"Father?"

"What?"

"I think a lot on you."

"And same on you, youth, never fret."

Jack put his arm about Nan Sarah and left the house. When they were out of the yard, the door was banged shut.

"Where can we go? What shall we do?"

"Come up, wife. It's a fine night to take some air. It's good for you, so they say. I know a place as'll suit us well. Soft now, love."

A clear, waning moon was in the sky, and they walked at Nan Sarah's pace towards Old Gate Nick between the high stones.

"Me legs are wrong," she said. "Moon hurts."

Her steps had begun to jerk, then sometimes dance, and sometimes she strode, and sometimes tottered. Jack held her firm and they rested often.

At Old Gate Nick they went along gentle Cats Tor and down the ridge.

"I do believe I can't go no further, Jack. Me back aches."

"No need, love. We're there."

They had come upon Thoon from above. He helped her down the side of the rock, took off his black goatskin coat and laid it on the shelf for her to sit, and held her close for warmth.

"I'm that spent," she said.

"Then rest, love. Jack shall watch you."

She put her head on his shoulder.

"Oh, bonny Bull," he whispered. "Bless us and keep us this night."

Thursbitch was silver below them.

Nan Sarah slept; but she twitched and her breathing was rough.

Jack was holding her now to stop her from falling off the rock as much as to comfort her. She was sweating, though her brow was a dry heat. Her limbs flexed. Yet she slept.

"Jack. I'm thirsty."

"Hush, love."

"I must drink."

"Let me settle you, so as you don't fall, while I fetch some in me hat."

"I brought Blue John. Me shawl."

Jack felt for the stone and took it. He moved Nan Sarah so that her back was held by the crevice in the middle of the hollow, and tucked her around with the goatskin.

"Bide still as you can, love. I'll be back directly."

He ran sideways down Catstair, on land so sheer that a trip would kill him; but each place for his foot shone in the light every step to the ford. He ran to Pearly Meg's and filled the cup. Then he ran back, scrambling up the steep, one hand on the slope, the other spilling not a drop.

Nan Sarah had slumped. He held her upright, and sat by her.

"Here, love, drink this; and I'll fetch you more."

He put the cup to her lips and she drank without pause until the cup was dry. Then he propped her, and set off again.

He was near the ford when he heard her scream. It was no small pain that cried. He ran. She lay out of the shelter. He lifted her. She screamed at every touch and move. "Jack! Jack! It burns! Jack! It burns! Burns! Burning!" Her body went into spasm stronger than he could hold and a stinking warmth flowed from her.

"Jack."

"Wife."

She was dead. She was dead, but her body had not done. He felt the spasm again and her legs and hips moved. Again. Again. Again.

Again. Again. Again. Again. He gathered all onto the goatskin. Then he stood. He looked up into the red eye of the Bull, with the moon in its horns, and he roared and lifted rocks from the ground and hurled them at the sky.

"You nowt! You nowt! False have you flummoxed me! You never said! You never said as this was yon night! You never said as poison was tonight!"

He flung the cup from him into the valley.

"Wife!"

Thoon answered: "Wife."

He picked up the goatskin in his arms and ran. He ran along the ridge, over Cats Tor to Old Gate Nick and Hog Brow Top, along by the high stones down to Saltersford.

He kicked at the door and banged with his head. Voices were on the other side. He kicked and banged and shouted, but no words. The door opened, and Mary stood there, Richard Turner beside her with his flintlock.

He held out the goatskin.

Mary put her candle aside and took the skin and opened it.

"Quick, Rutchart. A clean gown. Fetch blankets. More sticks. There's two on 'em; and they're breathing."

Jack picked up the goatskin from where Mary had dropped it and put it on.

"Jack has seen a black sun."

"Come in and wash you."

"Torn to bits in the wits of his mind. Left only the knowing heart. And the green leaves they grow rarely."

He stepped away.

"Snake and stone. They live for ever. And for why? They never care owt. And what is us but blood and soot?"

"Jack?"

"Jack? Him's a headless carcass and a nameless thing."

He went into the shippon and picked up a sledgehammer. He went up the lane to Jenkin. The pillar caught the light. He lifted the hammer and smashed it onto the face of the white rock. "Snake. Stone. Snake. Stone." He swung until Jenkin cracked and fell. "Snake. Stone. Snake. Stone." He pounded the shaft to lumps, the lumps to fragments. "Snake. Stone. Snake. Howl ye!" He threw the hammer at the moon, and fled.

24

"A question, Ian."

"Yes?"

"Am I still *compos mentis*? Legally?"

"In my opinion."

"Would you say that in court?"

"Yes."

"Thanks."

"Why do you ask?"

"Just checking."

"And?"

"I'm having the same dream every night, or nearly, or so it feels."

"I'm listening."

"It goes back to soon after I learned to read. Not the dream. It was a fairy tale. I can't remember what it was called or where I found it."

"It doesn't matter."

"It's about a Prince, who was so vain that he was interested only in himself and his clothes and looks."

"Tell me in the present tense."

"Why?"

"It'll help."

"Oh. We're doing Abreactive Therapy, are we?"

"Please, Sal."

"Anything you say, Ian. It's about a Prince who is so vain that he is interested only in himself and his clothes and how he looks. So his father has a round tower built for him, and the wall of the top room and the roof are made of alternate panels of mirror and window. The view from the windows shows all the world and the sky.

"The Prince loves the room and won't leave it. All he does is look at himself in the mirrors and at the reflections from every side. He never looks out of a window.

"The next day he's woken by a creaking sound. And the creaking wakes him every morning. He thinks nothing of it; then after several days he notices that the mirrors are becoming wider than the windows. Am I boring you, am I?"

"Far from it."

"Well, the Prince is chuffed with the bigger mirrors, and every morning he wakes at the creaking and goes to see how much more they have widened. This goes on until, one day, he thinks the mirrors are getting dirty, because he can't see himself clearly, so he sets about polishing the glass. But it makes no difference. Then he sees what's happening.

"The mirrors aren't dirty. It's the windows that are getting narrower and letting less and less light in. He tries to force the windows apart, but he can't. Outside, the sun is shining and he sees all the bright colours. And when he looks in the mirrors all he sees is a dimming reflection.

"Each day he presses his face against the mirrors, but he can see no more than his own self fading. Then there is one last creak, and the wall and roof become all mirror, and the Prince is alone in the dark. That's the story."

"What's the dream?" he said.

"I'm in that room, but I'm not the Prince. I'm me. The mirrors are what is now. The windows are what is going. There's no door. It's getting so bad that when I wake I'm scared to open my eyes. Would you still say I'm sane?"

"Of course you are sane. But it is significant."

"Obviously. I want you to explain more of it. I need help, Ian."

"I can't, Sal. It is your dream, not mine. It would not do any good if I were to suggest a meaning. It would be my response, not yours. Start by asking why it is this particular fairy tale you are turning to. What is in it that you need so much? Find that, and the dream will stop. In the meantime, there is no need to be scared."

"I knew that's what you'd say. You're infuriating. But thanks. I feel better for telling you and you not back away."

"Do you want to tell me again now?"

"Not now. I'm knackered."

"That is good, Sal."

"You have to say that."

"I do not."

"OK. So I can go to the next thing. I want you to make two promises."

"And what are they?"

"The first is that you'll give me plenty of warning before I reach the point where I can't think straight."

"I promise. What's the second?"

"I'll tell you that after you've kept the first."

"Fine."

"Why haven't you asked me what I'm up to?"

"It's none of my business, Sal. I shall find out when the time comes, presumably."

"You will."

"So that's all right."

"I used to think that you were a bit of a cold fish, you know."

"Perhaps I am."

"You're not. It's just one part of your nature. You're the only friend who has never shown any impatience with me over this thing, and never been irritated by my clumsiness. You don't talk down to me. You show no sense of pity. You don't hit back at my tantrums."

"Why should I? They are not meant. You forget so quickly that you can't get to the end of them as often as not."

She laughed. "There you go."

"How could I do otherwise? What would be the point? And haven't I always been like this? I thought I was consistent."

"Yes, but then, Ian, dear heart, it was as though you were refusing to engage. Observing from outside, but never joining in, in case you had to show emotion."

"Not at all. Just the opposite. It depends on how you view whatever we call reality. Is the fish in the sea, or is the sea in the fish?"

"That's mere bloody Jesuitical pyrotechnics, dodging the issue as usual."

"Is it? I don't mean it that way."

"Of course it is. And you know it. You always did try to get a rise out of people; find how gullible you could make them; see how far you could lead them by the nose, and see who ducked first. It used to piss me off, but now it is oh so refreshing. Such a change from: 'How are we today? Are we comfortable? What are we going to watch on television?' Forever the sodding plural. I want to shout: 'I don't know how you are today! I don't know whether you are comfortable! I do know that I am going to watch pretty futile pabulum! I am feeling lousy! This chair is fit only for the scrap heap! I am longing for some abrasive company!'."

"Do you ever say that?"

"Frequently."

"How do they react?"

"'Have we taken our medication?'."

"Oh, Sal!" The laughing drove the raven from the rock.

25

The last snow traced Thoon and the Tors, marking Catstair and the cattle gates. Light after winter was coming back into Saltersford.

Mary kept peering out through the windows.

"What's to do with you?" said Richard Turner. "Can a man not take a pipe o' bacca without you being up and down with your mither?"

"Don't you be three-cornered with me, Rutchart. There's a chap down yonder. He's been skulking in the lane and round about up bank all morning. Have you not heard the dogs?"

"Where? Let me see. Fecks, yay! We don't want his kind o' sort hereabouts."

He went to the door and opened it. Across the lane in Little Hall there was a man looking at the house. His hair and beard merged below his shoulders, and one hand was moving away from his side in a palsy.

"Hey! Shape for shift thisen! Else I'll raddle thi bones for thee!"

The man gestured with the palsied hand, and moved off towards Nab End. Richard Turner went back to his chair by the fire.

"If yon allsorts shows him again, see to it as you tell me. We don't want none o' them foreign parts."

"No need o' that," said Mary. "Here he comes."

"Right, master, right! Let's find what the dogs make on you." Richard Turner went to the yard. The dogs were barking. He opened the gate and whistled them out. "Come up! Fetch him!" They ran out into the lane. Richard Turner watched with Mary from the window of the houseplace.

The man stood still as the dogs approached.

"They'll have him," said Mary.

The man crouched before the pack. They leapt into his arms, licking his face, yelping, all their tails wagging. He had to stand, so that they did not knock him over. They were on their hind legs, paws on his back and chest, and he was ruffling their heads and necks.

"He's Jack!" Richard Turner ran into the lane. "Jack! Jack! Wherever have you been? See at the state you're in! Come thy ways, youth! Wash and change thisen!"

Only the black goatskin was the same. His hat was misshapen on his head, the band and feather gone. His satchel was stained with dirt and grease, his britches too, and rent. His stockings were torn, and his shoes gaped. His gaunt skin was as dark as his matted hair and beard. Salt was crusted round his mouth. His eyes shone, but they had changed. They were both beast and Jack.

"Come thy ways!"

He calmed the dogs and pushed them down. Then, without moving towards the house, he spoke in a hoarse voice.

"Rust, dust, tarbottle, bagpipolorum hybattell. Nettles grow in an angry bush. I saw a woman full of names and blasphemy. And the woman was bedight wi' gold, and held a cup in her hand full of abominations and filthiness of her abominations and filthiness of her fornication. And on her head was writ Mother o' Harlots, or some such."

He was holding the stick with the carved drum and bead, and spun it all the while.

Mary came out and went to him and took him by the arm.

"I'm sure as how there was. But you're home now, Jack."

"Woe unto us that we have sinned. For this us heart is faint. For this us eyes are dim. All along as how mount of Zion is desolate and foxes walk on it."

"Thee come thy ways."

"Tear off this garment as you wear; this cloak of darkness; this web of ignorance, this prop of evil, this bond of corruption, this living death, this walking corpse, this bury-hole as you carry. Beware the flesh into which you have entered, the path from which there is no return and from which all light is parted. For your veins, even your mortal veins, are the net wherein Satan shall trap you."

"We'll do that, Jack; never fret. But come thy ways now; there's a good youth."

"Do thorns prick today?"

"Fecks," said Richard Turner. "His tongue's going on wheels."

26

He sat at the top of the lane across from the stump of Jenkin and spun the wooden drum.

Tally Ridge came down from Pym Chair. "Is that you, Jack Turner? By, but you've been gone a while. And what a sight! You're that beshitten. What's to do wi' you?"

"Fetch folks," said Jack, not looking at Tally.

"Fetch folks? Whatever for?"

Jack did not answer. He turned the drum and stared at the stump.

Tally Ridge shook his head and went on his way. "Fetch folks. Ay, we'll do that. They'll want to see what sort o' notimaze you've turned out to be sin last back end."

Jack sat through the morning, not speaking, as the people began to drift towards Jenkin, and into the afternoon. They were quiet among themselves, muttering and whispering at what they saw and what he had become.

"Nay," said Sneaper Slack. "Get up wind on him. We could take a nest o' wasps wi' that one."

When enough were gathered, Jack stood, but continued the spinning.

"O ye unhappy men of Belial. I'm here to warn you of your torment, and of yon fires to come for you as walk in slippy places."

They looked at one another.

"Take heed, my brethren, I beseech you, for your labour for that meat as perishes and forget that meat as perishes not."

The women began to snicker.

"It is with grief I speak these things. Yet if I did not, the very stones would cry out."

"Ay. Stones, then," said Clonter Oakes. "And what can you tell us about him as smashed Jenkin?"

"It was the hand of God in his wrath as smote yon bethel of Satan, as his hand is ready to smite you all."

"Then how was it as one o' Turners' sledgehammers was found just where you're standing now, Jack?" said Tally Ridge.

Jack ignored him.

"God passed by me when I was polluted with innard filth, and let me live; He passed by me, and let me live so as I could fetch you news of His great anger against you, and to bruise the heads of snakes as they will bruise your heels. For you shall all, every one, be surely cast into yon flames, where the worm does not die, and the fire is not quenched. For you wicked shall go away into everlasting torment!"

"Give over," said Clonter. "We piss out bonfires, so what's the odds?"

"O deluded sinner. Think how it will be for you to dwell with burnings everlasting."

"Yay, but where shall your chap find enough sticks?"

Some of the children were crying.

"Ah, childer as are unconverted, do not you know as you are going down to Hell, to bear yon dreadful wrath of that God, who is now angry with you every day and every night? And women as are their mothers, will you as have neglected this precious season and have spent all your days in wickedness, will you know as how you are now come to such a dreadful pass in blindness?"

The women had fallen silent. But the men urged Jack on.

"Ay, youth! You tell 'em, and then!"

"Beware of Baccbus, yon Great Satan, you as are dead and barren in prayer. Lament and weep for miseries as shall come upon you; for the sword of God's word shall smite off the heads of them as he hates, even as this here idol was cut down. Therefore, let everyone now awake and fly from the wrath to come. Yon great wrath of Jehovah hangs over you. Haste and escape for your lives. Look not behind you. Escape to yon mountain, lest you be consumed."

There were shouts and cheers.

"Good lad, Jack!"

"A bonny tale!"

"Very well told!"

"Choice and all!"

Jack walked away down to Saltersford, the drum still whirling.

"By," said Sneaper Slack. "Yon effort beats Bull for laughs, and no error."

27

Edward had come over from Redmoor to help move the cattle up at the end of spring.

"Seems as how our Jack's back again from another on his jags."

As they climbed towards Shady, they could see the people gathered at Jenkin and hear their cries.

"Well, summat's back," said Richard Turner. "But whether or not it's our Jack is a question. Way that one's carrying on, he neither dies nor does."

"I heard chuntering soon as I left Redmoor," said Edward. "He's got to be put right, Father. He's been home long enough. Have you not tried reason?"

"Me, I've a farm to be run rather than listen to any more of his muckfoodle talk," said Richard Turner. "Reason! With that one? A man might as good go stop an oven wi' butter."

"I had hoped as how, once he was on jag again, he'd find his wits," said Edward, "seeing as we'd kept his beasts for him. But off he must go as if nowt had happened nor with a by your leave. And now his jags take longer and he fetches less; so what must he be doing, I ask ye, but mithering others same as here? And his childer. Has he been to Lomases to see 'em, or asked after 'em? He has not. It's as if they never were. And will he wash and keep himself? He will not. He's getten that ronk as a man can smell him afore hear his bells, when wind's right. I must tell you, Father, I reckon as you're being soft. Jack always did have the best end of the pig trough."

"Ay. Well."

"Show him who's master."

"It's not that easy, youth."

"Is it not? He's got us all at a tight rein, has Jack. And them as are down there now on their whirlybones, skriking and blahrting with him. Oh, they began at laughing when he first struck up, right enough; our Jack was quite the show. But by fits and gurds he's getten 'em eating out of his hand, so as they can't tell t'other from which. And who are they? Oakses, and Slacks, and Ridges, and Swindells, and Lomases, and Potts, and Lathams, and Adsheads. It seems there's nobbut Martha Barber won't have no truck wi' 'em. Who on us shall be next? There'll come a time when there'll be scarce any farming in this valley, for 'em all hill-hooting wi' Jack."

"Yay, but you don't know all as happened."

They moved the cattle along the Butts.

"I do know as he never did say nowt on how we'd kept his beasts and got feed for 'em all winter, let alone us selves. There were no thanks there. So what did happen, Father?"

"It's this road up. Soon as land man come, full on his talk of Thursbitch, I knew Bull wouldn't stand it. I knew as he'd turn nowty. And Bull and Jack are one folk, think on, at this time o' day. And Jack knew it. And he went and said sorry and as how he'd take it on his self to see right by Bull. But yon was a gate as he didn't know he was taking; and hasn't Bull called a bonny tune. First Nan Sarah, and now Jack. Bull has him on Belderstone now, right enough, and has pegged his een and peppered his chin good and proper."

"You never said, Father."

"It was between me and Jack."

"What's to be done, then?"

"Hold fast. That's what. Bull can bide while folks forget. It all comes round, in the long run, if we can thole while others learn to mind their ways and do things by rights again. It may not be in our time; but we must see. Bezonter. That's me jiggered for telling."

"Father, I never thought."

"You can think now."

"But what shall we do? How shall we thole? How shall we, then?"

"We'll build Jack a little ark," said Richard Turner. "For him and his brood chicks. And we shall fence it round, so as they can pick away to their hearts' content; and we can grow cabbage."

28

"Are you sure you're warm enough?"

"I'm fine. I like cold. I like wind. Stop fussing."

Showers were blustering with the sun.

"The cave will shelter us from this southeaster."

"Oh, groan. Here they come. Does nothing put them off?"

"Good afternoon!"

"Good afternoon. No, these are the hard men. This next lot are another matter."

A school group approached, close to the wall, although the wind drove against their exposed side. They each held the same map boards. No one was looking at anything but the ground ahead, their hoods pulled down to their eyes and their collars over their mouths. The mini-bus at Pym Chair was in sight, but they could not increase their pace. The walking had made them sullen. Only the teachers were chatting amongst themselves; and one kept hectoring the children with facts they would not hear.

"Good afternoon!"

"Good afternoon."

"Poor buggers," she said. "But I suppose it all helps towards something or other in the great educational scheme of things. Though I see no budding Ph.Ds there. No one appears to be exactly enthralled by the Todd Brook Anticline. They're shent. Ian? Mind if we prop the wall up for a moment? My legs are feeling the climb."

"Do you want to go back?"

"No, I do not, thank you very much. I'll tell you when that day comes."

They stopped at the hollow of Old Gate Nick. The way had been walled across, but was clear to see between the scarps above Saltersford and over the heather towards Goyt.

"On, on, on," she said, and pushed off from the wall with her poles. The bank of Cats Tor was steep out of the worn Nick. She slipped, but he was holding her by her belt and across the shoulders. "Sorry. Oh, damn it to hell. To hell and back. Sod it. Sod it. Sod it. Ian. I can't do this bit."

"You can. Fireman's lift. Hup."

He draped her as a bolt of cloth. Her arms hung, dangling the poles.

"Thanks. That was great."

"Are you comfortable?"

"Yes. Very."

"Then stay there. You're no weight."

"Put me down, Ian."

"No. This way, you don't have to have a social conscience, Doctor Malley."

She laughed, and he strode along Cats Tor, while she walked upside down backwards on the poles.

"Help!" she shouted as they were overtaken. "Abduction! Murder! Rape! Rapine!"

The walkers accelerated past, not looking, silent.

"We've cracked it!"

They continued along the ridge to the sawn-off telegraph pole in the fence. He lowered her onto the other side and climbed over.

"I'll walk now," she said. "I don't fancy being dumped in a bog."

They staggered across the short distance to the outcrop and sat on the flat bed of the recess, overlooking the valley.

"I said we'd be out of the wind."

They watched the patterns of light on Thursbitch and the silver showers driving.

"Fan. Tastic. This is my place," she said. "I could live here for ever. But I do live here. That's the odd thing. My thoughts aren't tunnelled to that obsessed clinical future. I'm not stuck in a bland room or zimmering around a garden. For God's sake, I'm not a botanist."

" It's because you're not under pressure."

"Weird. Normally, I could never say in clear what I've just said. It's those damned doctors and nurses. It's not their fault. At least, I hope it's not. They have to follow the book: 'Always formulate a question so that, if required, the patient can answer with a single negative or positive. To confront with the need to make complex decisions can lead to unnecessary distress.' That's one thing you do not forget when you read it, I can tell you. It's no basis for scintillating conversations. And when someone spins words so that you can say only X or Y, is it any wonder you sink into their ways? But here I'm with what I know: and remembering what I had for breakfast is no big deal any more."

"Carboniferous grits are more than cornflakes."

"Exactly."

"Speaking of which," he said, and opened his bag and took out the sandwiches, held her drink, and fed her.

"But I do understand how fortunate I am, Ian. Sometimes I do."

They watched the valley.

"Ian?"

"Yes?"

"You keep looking at me."

"Sorry."

"Why?"

"I don't mean to."

"And differently."

"Sorry."

"Ian! Stop apologising! All I want is a straight answer to a simple observation! You're such a bloody Pygmalion and so smug! 'Look what I'm doing. I give up my precious time for a terminal case. I go to infinite pains to keep my composure. Look at me. Don't you admire my objectivity? Am I not the epitome of the empathising professional at work? She sits there with a face as yard as a fiddle-stick, thpewing abuthe and I never flinch.' How I dethpithe roo! Roo mothionleth cold-fingered wakord! Where are the bells? Can you hear them, Ian?"

"No."

"Tinkling. Listen."

"I can't hear them."

"I can. Somewhere near. Now they've gone. Never mind. It's marvellous."

"Why did you never marry, Sal?"

"What?"

"Just an idle thought."

"Like hell it is. If you must know, I got tired of massaging male egos that couldn't see any point in what I was doing with my own work. And thank God for that. At least I don't have to face up to what I might have left to any kids. But you skedaddled into your seminary PDQ, didn't you? Talk about *fait accompli*, mate in one. Or not, in this case."

"That was not the reason, Sal."

"If it wasn't, it was a damned good substitute. Your chum Ignatius is a pretty effective bouncer. Or is celibacy inherited, too? That's a joke. Did you love me?"

"Sal. Stop. You know that is the one aspect that must not come into this. Do not even think of it. If you do, we cannot meet. Any where, any how. Certainly never alone here. I could be struck off on both spiritual and medical ethical grounds. It is a subject that does not and must not apply."

"That's the first time I've seen you panic in twenty years."

"You should know better than to do this, if here really does mean what you say it means."

"I apologise."

They were silent again.

"Don't twitch, Ian. You're as bad as me."

He stood, and gazed out over the valley, and was quiet. Then he sat and took hold of both her hands.

"Sal. Look at me. No. Look at me."

"Oh. Eye contact. Of course."

"Your neurologist has written to say that you can't be treated where you are any longer. You'll have to go into hospital next month."

"How long?"

"That long."

"Where?"

"Manchester."

"No."

"The last scan showed a crucial deterioration."

"But you promised."

"I did."

"You promised you would tell me before I lost my wits."

"It is not your mind, Sal. It is your body. The motor systems are critical, and you are going to need more support than they can give you at the Home."

"Thanks, Ian."

"We can still come here."

"I'm glad you told me. I mean. I'm glad it was you."

"Now it's my turn to thank."

"You made another promise."

"I haven't had to keep the first one yet."

"This changes things. I may need to activate the second before the first."

"You've not told me what it is."

"Dear heart, methinks you already know."

29

Richard Turner and Edward stood before the building. It was new in the sun; every fresh cut block of stone, every roof slate, twinkled and glittered. The glass of the windows shone. Whitewash was unblemished on the door in the gable end.

"By, yon's fine as Filliloo," said Richard Turner. "But it's to be hoped we see nowt on land man for a year or three, else Jack may have a roof o'er his head, but we shall likely not."

"Have you done the right thing, Father?" said Edward. "Are you certain sure?"

"I believe so, youth. I do believe it. There's no going back on it now, anyroad, is there? But we're ploughing a narrow adlant, I'll grant ye."

"When I see at it," said Edward, "and then see at land and how it's cost, yon clack box is no bonny thing, but two bays o' beggary; and ruination of Saltersford. There's not a ditch been scoured, nor a drain rodded, nor a shippon nor a house roof stopped gen rain and snow sin this effort began. And when roof's shotten, house is gone. There's places no more nor wind holes for want of new raddle and daub in the wall frame."

"Do you think as how I need telling of that?" said Richard Turner.

"And see at the kyne, Father. We scarce got one bite of hay for winter, all on account of mither for fetching purlin timbers. And Bean Croft's seen no liming."

"Nay, Edward. That'll do. You're speaking feart o' far enough now.

By hulch and stulch, we'll live till we die, if the pigs don't eat us. And I did mix a gallon of bull's blood wi' the mortar. So it's not all wrong road. Look ye. Chimney draws a treat."

The first fire had been lit, and a white smoke rose into the sky. They turned their backs on the shining build and went down the lane through the sorry land.

Jack was sitting in the houseplace, talking to himself, and turning the bead and drum. Mary had put on her Nottingham lace cap.

"Folks are ready for you, Jack."

He did not answer, but stood and left the houseplace into the lane. Richard Turner, Mary and Edward followed him back to the glint of stone. There was the smell of fresh timbers and newly cut blocks, and of whitewash and strewn rushes. The box pews were filled with silent people, except for one pew bigger than the rest. Here Sneaper Slack and Clonter Oakes sat. Richard Turner and Edward sat with them, and Mary found a place with the women.

Jack mounted the steps of the pulpit in the middle of the far gable, and looked at the people. He held the silence. Everyone watched as he turned his head to the walls and ceiling, then down to the pews.

"So," he said. "God has spared you to build this house and tabernacle to His glory in this here one thousand and seven hundred and thirty-fourth year sin yon Vulgar Dionysian Years of Christ, and five thousand six hundred and eighty year from yon Creation of this World. It will help you not at all. Your labours are as nowt in the scale of your evils. He has permitted you to do this thing so as you may better hear of terrors as await you in the judgments of Hell."

There were moans.

"It avails you nowt to lament. Skrike ye, O ye foredoomed. Think you to escape His great wrath, His almighty anger? It cannot be, seeing as how God, as knows all things and can do no wrong, has seen from the start as how you, His creatures as He made, would turn to Sin;

and of for that He is angered. Therefore, seek no mercy, but prepare
to die in the fire as dies not."

His voice was soft. Weeping broke out among the people.

"I see you now, you agen hearthplace yonder, hutching and
thrutching so as to be near its warmth. I think on as how this night
of the year you would light your bone fires and jump in 'em. Think
you as them are the flames of Hell? No. No more nor a grain of sand
to a mountain. No. Much less nor that. For bone fires you can jump
through, and when you are warmed by yon hearth you can shift away.
But in Hell you can neither jump nor shift. You shall be bound for
evermore and laid on griddles as are never quenched, and for you
there shall be no shifting."

"Hallelujah!"

"Yay. Well may you call upon His name. But even now you do not
ketch on. Draw near. Hearken ye to the words I have to tell of torments
for to come."

He leaned forward and beckoned them towards him with both
hands, and lowered his voice. The air had lost its sweetness.

"God holds you over the pit of Hell, of fire, of brimstone, same as
He holds a spider or some such loathsome insect. He abhors you and
is dreadfully provoked. His wrath towards you burns same as that fire.
He looks upon you as worthy of nowt else but to be cast in yon pit.
He is of purer een nor can bear to have you in his sight."

"Amen!"

"Yay. You are ten thousand times more abominable in His een nor
the verymost hateful snake. You have offended Him; and yet it is nobbut
his hand as holds you from falling every moment into the fiery pit.
It is nobbut else as kept you out of Hell last night, so as you were
suffered to wake again in this world after you shut your een."

"Glory!"

"Jehovah!"

"Yay. And there is no reason to be given as why you did not drop into Hell when you got up this morning, but that the hand of God has held you."

"Blessed be!"

"Yay. There is no other reason to be given as why you have not gone to Hell when you sat yoursen down here, provoking His pure een by your wicked manner of attending His solemn worship. Ay, there's nowt else as can be given as the reason for why you do not at this very moment drop down into Hell."

Women and men were screaming and fainting. But Jack drew them in further, his voice a whisper.

"O Sinners. Consider what fearful danger you are in. It is a great furnace of wrath, a wide and bottomless pit, full of fire of wrath, as you are held over by the hand of that God whose wrath is provoked and incensed as much agen you as agen many already in Hell. You hang by a slender thread, wi' flames of divine anger flashing about it, and ready every moment to singe it, and burn it asunder. And you have nowt to lay hold on to save you; nowt to keep off the flames of wrath, nowt of your own, nowt as you ever have done, nowt as you do to make God spare you one moment."

Some were trying to get out of the pews, but could not open the doors in their panic.

"You cannot escape. You shall be same as burning lime, as thorns cut up in ovens shall you be burnt. And you must suffer it to all Eternity. There shall be no end to this misery. You must wear out long ages, many and many ages, with this almighty and merciless vengeance. And then, when you have so done, you shall know as all is but a point of what remains. Your punishment shall indeed be without end."

Jack put his hand over the edge of the pulpit. Pain struck into his palm. A bee was embedded in the flesh. He lifted it close to his eyes.

"Nay. Not you. Not you. Never you. Never you as first fed." He held the bee and turned it to unwind the sting from his hand.

He was sweating, and his head thumped with the charge of the Bull.

Jack got down from the pulpit, his step unsure on the lurching wood. The people were silent. The air became the smell of a hive, and a noise of wings.

He opened a light of the window, still looking close.

"From death to death she goes." Crom's tongue filled his mouth and rasped as he forced it to speak.

He raised his hand to the window. The bee flew out into the valley and scents of flowers. He looked around the walls and at the people.

"From life to life."

He saw them through a dark web of holes with six sides, and in each hole was a face that he did not know. He tried to back away, but he was against rock; and against rock he dragged himself. No one moved or made a sound. They watched the black coat slide along the white wall.

He put his knuckle in his mouth, against the stone tongue, and bit through, knowing only the Bull's truth, the wisdom of the Bee.

30

They took Jack by the arms and led him down the lane. He did not speak.

Mary went into the houseplace, and Richard Turner and Edward stripped him and sat him in the brook. They cut his hair and beard and nails and scraped and scoured his flesh, and then Edward went to bring him clean clothing, and they dressed him, cleansed and bound the wound, and took him to the fire. He sat, shivering, gazing at the flames. Mary gave him a cup of hot raspberry vinegar with honey and salt. He drank.

Still no one spoke.

"I never once was stung by a bee," said Jack.

He was silent again. His eyes moved, watching in the flames, and his face showed what he saw. Mary looked at Edward and nodded, and they left the room. Richard Turner stayed at the table and followed the story in Jack's eyes.

Jack lifted his head.

"When a man sees on his hand his own living honey-eating sen, maker of what was and what must come, she never looks to hide from him."

"All's well, youth," said Richard Turner.

"Her as was born afore fire, afore water was born, her as knows every mortal thing and things as never die. Her as we know in the cave of us hearts, and see sitting now."

"Ay."

[144]

"But what were yon lot huzzing there? What wanted they to have to do wi' me?"

"You're home, youth. Never fret."

"Outside is mad. Mad is Outside.

"And Great Mortality. It didn't take."

"What didn't take?" said Jack.

"Do you not recollect?"

Jack shook his head.

"Nobbut pockets."

"Where were you gone all winter?"

Jack shook his head.

"Fury of the black goatskin. It took me. And Fury of the black goatskin. It fetched me. I did tread an iron gate. I did see horrors. I did eat me childer. Me own childer."

"Nowt of the sort," said Richard Turner. "Lomases were breeding, and they took 'em in to rear."

"Outside is mad. Mad is Outside. You do not see Them. I do."

"As you please."

"I did eat me childer."

"You did not."

"Then where's their mother? I keep thinking as I ketch her through the side of my een. But when I look she's gone."

"Try pockets, youth."

"Pocket. Ay. Pockets." Jack stared into the fire again, and Richard Turner watched. "Pockets. Pockets. I ketch 'em. I do. I do that. And summat. Biggening Brom. Petticoat. Honey. Blue Nan? Grallus. Wife!"

Jack surged from the fire and flung himself onto Richard Turner. Richard Turner held him, cradled him, felt the wracking of his strength as his body cried out. It was the cry of beast and man, shaking the houseplace, mortal and undying. Richard Turner held. The body thrashed and slowed and was still.

"I've been lost in the star-sodden wits of me mind, Father. Left nobbut an unknowing heart."

"Yay, but you're back now, youth."

"How must I mend? Bull shall be vexed, and Crom."

"Then you'd best ask 'em. It's your time o' day now, none else's. But tha conner fart gen thunder, think on; and bliss in this world it is a seldom thing."

"All the crueltiness I've done at Saltersford and at folks."

"Thee never you mind that," said Richard Turner. "That's for us to mend. And what you've done is mebbe Bull's road as he's chosen for us. Though I see no road round what's-his-face, land man, and his big ways. He'll do as he pleases, that one. But Bull's bigger nor ways, and bigger nor all. Now folks have gotten their little ark, their minds are not on Bull. No matter o' that. Ranting's nobbut cluntish talk, as any a one can do. I'll keep watch on 'em, so as they don't grow nowty. And one thing about stone. It keeps in. As long as they've got yon for chelp on, they'll happen not spoil the land. And then we must next breed it out on 'em. Nay, youth. It's for you to addle more. You must pay Bull full dole, and lay Nan Sarah to her peace, and set the stars by rights. Night's older nor day."

"I never ought to have chucked the grallus. There was that much hurt. Now it's done. Happen it's for others."

"Happen."

"Where's corbel bread for opening een and ears and tongue?"

"Where it's always kept," said Richard Turner. "You picked plenty last back end; and though it's a bit over fresh, to my mind, I don't doubt but what you'll thole."

"Why did you have to break Jenkin, Father?"

"Why me, are you asking?"

"Ay."

"I can't rightly answer you there, youth. It's a question. But what's done's done; and that's the top and bottom of it."

"Me head's going round like cocks and hens."

"It seems as you've a whealy mile ahead yet," said Richard Turner.

Jack lifted the bag from above the mantle beam and took out a cap and stem. They were dry, but still spongy. He took another, chewed and swallowed, using the last of the raspberry vinegar. Then, without speaking again, he went out and climbed up the Butts, over the brow and down into Thursbitch.

It was the end of a day of sun and showers. The black goatskin had not been cleaned, but he wore it against the wind. As he passed by Lankin he glimpsed a man on the ridge walking towards Thoon, something draped over his shoulder. Jack went to sit by Bully Thrumble and waited.

The sun did not sing, and he heard no cloud bells. The brook flowed by.

He waited. The stone was hard against his back. "Walk and do. Walk and do. Walk and do till all is done." He sat.

"Old Bouchert. Old Bouchert."

Nothing moved but a raven down the sky.

"O sweet Bull. O noble Bull. O worthy Bull. O bonny Bull."

He sat and waited, and saw no answer.

"O Bull, as lives on hill tops. Lord over all as close the eye. Your step full of honey. In your highmost step is honey. O Bull with mighty voice. Mask of Bull, kindled for beauty. O Bull striding the sky, shine down. For there is nowt as you are not."

There was no answer, but a darkness grew, greater than the light.

Jack rose and went down from Thrumble. He saw only what was black in the valley: the shales, the shadows. All else was a blur.

Then, as he came towards the finger of Lankin, he heard a voice out of Thoon.

"Turn."

It was the strong voice of a woman.

He stopped and looked. He could not see. "Nan Sarah?" No answer. "Nan Sarah!"

He left the track and stumbled and scrambled up Cats Tor to the ridge. The sun was setting and, with the dusk, his sight grew clearer. He moved along the bog. A man came towards him. When they met, they looked into each other's eyes, faltered, but did not speak. Each walked with a driven gait. Jack hurried to Thoon. "Nan Sarah?" Thoon was empty.

Richard Turner was waiting in the yard in the last of the light.

"Well, youth?"

"Nowt. I reckon as how I was too previous with yon corbel bread."

"Or was it you, Jack?"

"Bull was sulky, anyroad. He neither gave nor told."

"Or you didn't hear?"

"I thought, once, I did. But it was nowt. I did see a chap, though. And that was queer."

"How?"

"He was up Cats Tor, going for Pym Chair; and I was going for Thoon. We passed each other as close as I am to you, but in a bit of a clatter, like; so we didn't speak. But I looked at him. He had an odd-strucken sort of a twist to his face, full of grief and good. I swear as I saw a broken man, but one as could mend. And I swear, Father, I never did see a happier man. And he looked at me."

"And what did this chap see, Jack?"

"How should I know what he saw?"

"I'm thinking: were you not hearing Bull? Did this chap see same as you? Did he see a broken man as could mend?"

31

"Dear heart, methinks you already know."

"I don't, Sal."

"Bed wheels."

"What about them?"

"The first time I was in hospital, for tests, I kept looking at the wheels on the beds. They were quiet and watching. Then they'd rattle away. But they always came back, and be there, looking at me, waiting, day and night. When I left hospital I knew they were still there. They were in no hurry. And when I went in again, there they were. Now they know I'm coming, and this time they'll have me."

"What's the second promise?"

"I know what I'm saying, Ian. It's so hard that you don't have to answer. If you do answer, you must tell me the truth."

"You have my word."

"What is it, when the time comes, that will see me off?"

He put the back of his hand against her cheek.

"The most common causes of death are either dysphagia or the result of an opportunistic invasion, usually pneumonia."

"So it's choke or drown."

"It is."

"Thanks. I'm sorry I put that on you, but I had to know."

"If you want it, I shall be there with you."

"No, Ian. It won't come to that. I'm a coward. I shall go through the windows before they're too narrow and while there's still light."

~~~~~~~

He squeezed her hand and looked away.

"I'm a coward, Ian. I'm scared of the dark. I don't want the mirrors without the sky."

> "Salt seasons all things,
> Said Solomon the Wise;
> And him as gets a good wife
> He gets a goodly prize.
> Him as gets a wrong un,
> He falls into a snare;
> And Old Nick plucks him by the neck,
> As Mossy ketched his mare."

Jack climbed from Sooker and the snow was drifting. He held Jinney's reins to lift her. They passed Ormes Smithy, up Blaze Hill and along Billinge Side. The wind was full in their faces and the horses were trying to tuck into the bank for shelter, but Bryn kept them from shoving their panniers against the rocks. Now it was dark and the snow was swarming into his lanthorn and he could not see for the whiteness.

They crossed the four-went-way and began the drag up Pike Low. By Deaf Harry, Jinney reared. Jack shortened the rein and patted her neck and shoulder.

"Nay, nay, lass. Don't you take boggart now. Yon's a high stone, that's all. He can't hurt you. He can't move, choose what Tally Ridge'll say. Well, not tonight he won't."

He braced for the top of Pike Low.

"Blood and elbows! Oh, what a world. What a world. Summer hangs in a bag tonight; it does that. But we shall fettle it, shan't we? We shall and all." He led the train down from Pike Low by Drakeshollow; the wind and the snow still in his face. They climbed up Ewrin Lane and over Waggonshaw Brow. As he passed through the farmyard at Buxter Stoops, he saw Martha Barber at the curtain sack of her window.

"Is it you, Jagger Turner?"

"Ay, but it is, Widder Barber!"

"I thought I heard. Will you come thy ways?"

"Nay, Missis. But thank ye. If I let this lot melt I'd starve to death."

"Hast any piddlejuice about you for such a time?"

"I have and all. Good to make a cat speak and a man dumb. Pass us your jug, Missis, then get that down you, and you'll be as frisky as a tup in a halter."

"I always say as how there never has been nowt like your piddlejuice, Jagger; and that's a fact!"

"Ay, Missis! If you're on the road all hours in these hills, you must be fit for owt, or you'll find it's when bum hole's shut, fart's gone. It's there, you know. Oh, ah. When bum hole's shut, fart's gone."

They laughed on either side of the door.

"Give us a tune, Jagger! I feel a little ditty coming on me and I've a flavour for to sing it."

"Nay, Widder Barber. I must be getting down bank, and me beasts need their rest."

He saw her shadow. She was hopping and began to dance for Jenkin. Her voice was uncertain at first, but then it broke forth with a strength that not even the wind could quell.

"I must be getting down bank, Widder Barber! Wind's in Thoon's eaver, and me beasts'll be bangled if they're not moving!"

Martha Barber was now leaping in her dance; her head kecked backwards. The hollering wind took her voice from him, but the song was in the storm itself and came to him out of Thoon's very own mouth.

"The next great joy of Mary Anne
    It were the joy of seven:
    To see her own son little Jack

Reap up the stars of heaven;
Reap up the stars of heaven and make
Of them the golden Bee.
Euoi! Euoi! Io! Euoi!
Through all Eternity!"

"How will you do that, Sal?"

"Get out? I'll find a way."

"You know where I have to stand on this."

"Of course. I'm not asking you for anything."

"Are you hoarding pills? A stomach pump is not a pleasant experience."

"No. They're wise to that one. I'll find a way."

"You won't, Sal. You can't. You are not strong enough; physically."

"I must. It's my choice."

"Please reconsider. We can make all experience positive. We cannot know what will happen."

"I always did think you lot were a bunch of sado-masochists. Why should I have to put up with this longer than I need because some mediæval mentalities have nothing better to do than to take odds over angels on pins? I'm the one in the bed, remember. And I'd rather you didn't sit on it while you're comparing mattresses."

"In an ideal world – "

"Oh no. Please not that. It is not an ideal world."

"What would you want?"

"If you must know, I would stay here. Here is my place of understanding. 'And every stone and every star a tongue. And every gale of wind a curious song.' At school. I remember."

"Eternity?"

"Your kind? I find that queasy. Where's it all going to end? I ask. I'd be happy just to let my fingernails grow."

He stood, and walked on the sheer edge of the path and looked down at the confluence of the ford.

"My hypocritic oath," he said.

> "The next great joy of Mary Anne,
> It were the joy of nine:
> To see her own son Little Jack
> Pluck up the bilberry fine;
> Pluck up the bilberry fine to give
> Himself to thee and me.
> Euoi! Euoi! Io! Euoi!
> Through all Eternity."

Jack hauled his way back along Ewrin Lane towards Buxter Stoops. The bend near the top told him where to turn off to find the pillar of Osbaldestone in the white bees of snow. He swam to it and sat next to its strength, facing Thoon. He pulled his hat down against the blizzard and was still.

The wind about the stone spoke to him. "Towards the place into which you enter, the path from which there is no return, all light is withdrawn."

"Get off with your bother," said Jack. "You shall pass, and then we shall make a bonny moon and a laughing sky."

A warm wetness came under his hat. The dog licked his face.

"Now then, Bryn. You've been quick. Did you see 'em home? There's a good lad." The dog lay next to him and he patted it. "And what did I say? What did I tell you?" The wind had dropped. He pushed up his hat. The cloud was passing, and stars floated in the gaps.

"Now, Bryn. We have a job to do tonight. We have and all. We must put the stars and moon to rights. How's that, you say? Well, times have been a terrible rough auction of late, have they not? I recollect 'em all, the good wi' the bad, and every word true. The reason is, the sky's slippy; and every so often yon moon and stars get out of sorts, and it's given to folks same as us to fettle 'em and put 'em back on their high stones. And what wi' yon caper at Jenkin, and land man promising all sorts, Bull needs a hand, a bit of a hutch up, to set him back in his place; else each night of winter we can't see the grandest tale as is ever told in these parts, or any other, I shouldn't wonder: the tale as shows as how Bull shall never die, choose what ranters and land man do.

"And how shall we fettle, you ask me? Corbel bread. Yon's the truth of corbel bread, and why we always gather it up each back end down along the saltways and fetch it here. Corbel bread; same as tonight."

The sky had cleared.

"See at Nick."

A small cluster of stars rose from Old Gate Nick.

"Yon Bees are on Bull's shoulder. They're there to watch o'er him and feed him honey. Now see at Cats Tor."

To the right of the Tor shoulder, a red star showed.

"There's his eye, Bryn. It must ever peep out of yonder first, to see as all's well. And now he's seen, up he comes, sithee, to look on us. Isn't that a bonny sight, him with his highmost step?

"And now look ye at him proud above Thoon. But Thoon's a two-folk rock, it is that: a place of heaming and of dying. Yon's the bury-hole in life and life in the bury-hole. It is that. And now who's that coming out of there? This Big Chap with his club. He's after Bull; for he's the very cut-throat of cattle.

"But Bull sees him, and up he climbs to get rid. And the Big Chap's thrutching his belt out of Thoon; so he'll not be held long. Bull had best be doing. And now he's at his highmost, and the Big Chap's out and walking the ridge. And now he's striding into the sky off Shining Tor; and look ye; there's Old Goibert coming from Tor, but he's under the Big Chap's feet, and the Big Chap hasn't seen him. But, oh dear! What must Bull do now?

[154]

"And look ye! The Big Chap's getten a Dog, same as you, and he's been hid aback of Tor, and he's seen Old Goibert and he's going for him!

"But I'll tell ye what shall happen, though it won't happen this minute. Bull's going to nip down t'other side of Andrew's Edge to have a quiet crack wi' Crom in his sleep, and the Big Chap will think as he's getten him. But no. He'll ketch his foot above Long Clough, and down he'll plump. Same wi' Old Goibert. He'll drop in the grass, and the Dog'll never find him there. While Bull shall sneak round under Pike Low to peep at Cats Tor tomorrow night. As long as he peeps at Cats Tor, land man can never catch him. And that's a fact.

"And Deaf Harry, sithee, on Pike Low. He's watching the North Star again, at last, after ever so long and ever so many years of being wrong road. And all's well.

"We have done, Bryn. Bull's in his sky above Thoon, look ye. O bonny Bull. And all along of corbel bread."

Jack sat against Osbaldestone and saw the moon in the horns of the Bull. He was faint with effort, but warm, and he did not shiver.

> "The last great joy of Mary Anne
>   It were the joy of ten:
>   To see her own son little Jack
>   Afire wi' flame, and then
>   Afire wi' flame of corbel bread
>   Unlapping from the tree.
>   Euoi! Euoi! Io! Euoi!
>   Through all Eternity."

Ian came back and sat with her and put his arm around her and held her hand.

"You are right."

"What does that mean?" she said.

"I shall stay with you. Here. Now."

"Ian, you can't. I won't let you. It would destroy you. It's against everything you've ever lived by."

"That is for me to deal with."

"No. Even I can't be so selfish."

"I am the selfish one," he said. "You have called into question all that I had come to accept without hesitation or consideration. And I have no answer."

"I've lost you your Faith."

"No. But you may have found me some Grace."

"You have never made me cry before."

He stroked the hair outside her helmet.

"This is where you feel the need to be. You hold here to be sentient. It is only proper for this place to take you."

"You're talking as the priest."

"My particular Mafia does tend towards the œcumenical. For you it is a religious experience. The doctor in me can tell you hypothermia is kind: kinder than choking or drowning."

"I can't handle this. I wasn't expecting it."

"But is it what you want?"

"Yes."

"Are you sure?"

"I'm sure. And. Thanks. Keep the cup. It must mean something."

"It must."

"Right, then."

"Do you want a drink?"

"Yes."

"Do you want to eat?"

"No."

"I shall hold you."

"No. Ian, I feel such an ungrateful shit. But because you're right about this place, it would be wrong for you. I need to meet it myself; to find whatever's here for me. I shall dance till I swarm. What I'm saying is: please go. As one last gift, please go. I know how it sounds, but the feeling is the opposite, my dearest dear."

He kissed the top of her helmet.

"Ian. Do not look back. Whatever else you do with your life, do not look back."

"I love you, Sal."

"You always have. Turn."

He pulled himself from the rock and walked. He walked over the blanket bog and the cotton grass. He reached the point where the shoulder of Cats Tor began to hide the outcrop. He stopped.

She was not in the cave. She had got herself out onto the slab. She stood, leaning forward on her poles, her right foot in the print, striding above the valley. She had shed her helmet and her hair was free. He walked to the north.

"Eh up."

Light had appeared in Thoon, and grew as it left the cave and broke into points that formed as they moved across Thursbitch towards Jack, not in the sky but of the sky, clustered as the Bees, but golden and no shape that he had ever known of stars. The light drifted and changed; and he saw.

"Nan Sarah."

Her spun form grew above him, and, smiling, sank down. He lifted his face to hers, and she set her foot beside him as they kissed.

"Wife."

He laughed, holding her for a moment for ever. She smiled that they would not part, though her shape of light drew back into Thoon.

"Wife."

He looked out across the snows of Thursbitch, and his jagger's heart saw peace, through Nan Sarah's peace, at last.

"Bryn. If I'm to rest tonight in this flowery valley, tell them to put me in me own fold, so as I'm close to you. Then, tell them, put at me head a pipe of hornbeam, for sweetness; a pipe of holly, for sadness; a pipe of oak, for wildness. Then when the wind blows it must play. And tell them in good truth as how I wed the wench of this world; and a star fell.

"Tell them as how Sun and Moon held crown for me; as how Cats Tor and Shining Tor were me parsons, quickthorns me witness; and all to the singing of a thousand brids and the sky my torches."

And out over Thoon above Bully Thrumble the high lord hanging holy under heaven. And Crom asleep in the ground.